A LIFETIME TOGETHER

BY

MELINDA FAURE

Copyright Page

A Lifetime Together: The Story of Emma and Ethan
By Melinda Faure

Publisher's Note:
This is a work of fiction. Names, characters, places, and incidents are products of the author's imagination or are used fictitiously. Any resemblance to actual events, locales, or persons, living or dead, is entirely coincidental.

Published by Melinda Faure
South Africa

ISBN 978-0-6398437-7-3

Cover Design by: Melinda Faure
Interior Formatting by: Melinda Faure

First Edition

Printed in South Africa

Contents

Preface

In the quiet moments of life—amid the laughter, tears, dreams, and even heartbreak—there exists a love that endures. It is a love that withstands the test of time, growing stronger and deeper with every passing season. This story captures that journey—the story of Emma and Ethan, two souls whose love begins as a quiet ember and grows into a steady flame, lighting their path through life's winding road.

Their journey is one of rediscovery, resilience, and unwavering commitment—a testament to the beauty of choosing love, again and again, even in the face of uncertainty. From the early spark of youthful romance to the quiet, steadfast companionship of later years, Emma and Ethan's story reflects life's highs and lows. It celebrates what it truly means to share a life with someone.

In a world that often glorifies the fleeting, their journey reminds us of the quiet power of what lasts—the beauty of building a life brick by brick, memory by memory. Their love, far from perfect, is honest, enduring, and ever-growing. As their family blossoms and new chapters unfold, that love becomes a legacy, passed down like a well-loved story whispered across generations.

This book is not just a story of romance, but a meditation on family—on the bonds that hold us together, and the grace we offer each other as we navigate life's ever-changing terrain. It is a reminder that love is not merely a feeling, but a series of choices, a quiet vow repeated daily, and ultimately, the gift of walking alongside someone through every season.

May Emma and Ethan's journey inspire you to cherish the love you hold, to embrace the beauty within life's imperfections, and to find joy in the small, tender moments that give a life its meaning.

Welcome to their story.

Chapter 1: The Letter

The scratch of pen against paper echoed through the room as Emma paused mid-sentence, her fingers frozen and her breath catching with the weight of a memory as her mind drifted once again to the past. It was a rainy evening in London, and the soft patter against her office window seemed to mirror the melancholy that had settled in her heart. Work had become her refuge, filling the hours that might otherwise have been spent thinking about what she'd lost.

For the most part, Emma was content. She'd built a respectable career as an editor, lived in a charming flat near Covent Garden, and had friends she could count on. But none of that filled the ache lingering deep inside her—the quiet whisper in her heart, reminding her of how, once, it had belonged to someone who had slipped away.

It was Ethan—the boy from her final year at Whitestone High. He had been everything to her: her confidant, her partner in all the teenage adventures they could dream up, and her first taste of real love. But like so many young romances, theirs had faded in the wake of separate universities, career ambitions, and the demands of adult life.

She had dated others, of course. Some relationships had been comfortable, even promising. Others had left her more wounded than she cared to admit. Some had been decent men; others had left her wounded and disappointed. But no one ever filled that same space. Now, as her thirties stretched ahead with a slow, inevitable loneliness, she found herself thinking about Ethan more than ever.

Emma glanced at her calendar, noting a reminder in the corner: High School Reunion. The ache in her chest tightened—was it hope or fear? Either way, the thought of going stirred something long-buried, Whitestone, 7 PM. She had been on the fence about going. What if Ethan was there? What if he wasn't? The idea of seeing him again made her heart pound with a nervous thrill that felt entirely too reckless.

As if on cue, her phone vibrated with a message. Her best friend, Lucy, always seemed to know when she needed a nudge.

Lucy: Have you thought about what you're wearing on Saturday? ;)

Emma smiled at the screen. Lucy knew exactly what this reunion meant to her, even though Emma hadn't dared to say it out loud.

Emma: I haven't even decided if I'm going!

Lucy: Stop it! You know you have to. It's fate. You haven't seen Ethan in over ten years, and you know you want to. What if he's single? What if he's still waiting for you?

Emma's cheeks flushed. The idea was absurd. Ethan was probably married, settled somewhere in a quiet suburb, living a completely different life. But the hopeful part of her—the part that still believed in love stories and happy endings—wanted to believe in that "what if."

The night of the reunion came faster than she'd expected. Emma found herself standing in front of her mirror, a fitted black dress hugging her curves, her hair elegantly pinned back. She stared at her reflection, half-expecting to see the younger girl she once was. Her heart beat wildly as she slipped on her heels, doubting for the hundredth time whether this was a good idea.

When she arrived at the hotel hosting the reunion, the sound of laughter and soft music filled the room, immediately bringing back a rush of memories. She scanned the crowd, recognising old friends, acquaintances, and familiar faces, but her gaze kept drifting, searching for someone she wasn't sure would be there.

And then she saw him.

Ethan stood across the room, looking just as she remembered but older, the same dimple creasing his left cheek when he smiled—a detail that once made her heart flutter in high school corridors, his features sharper, his frame stronger. He was laughing with a group of former classmates, but, as if sensing her presence, he turned, their eyes locking across the crowded room. For a moment, neither of them moved, time seeming to freeze as a thousand unsaid words passed between them.

Emma's heart raced as he started towards her, a slow, confident smile spreading across his face. When he reached her, his eyes softened, a hint of wonder in his gaze.

"Emma," he said, his voice a low murmur that sent a thrill down her spine. "I was hoping I'd see you here."

"Hi, Ethan," she replied, her voice barely more than a whisper. All her fears, doubts, and insecurities seemed to melt away in his presence. It felt as if no time had passed, as if they were still those two young people, full of hope and endless dreams.

Chapter 2: Reaching Back

The familiar scent of his cologne drifted over her as they stood together, neither quite sure where to begin. Ten years stretched between them, both a chasm and a bridge, each memory vivid yet softened by time. She recalled the way he used to tap his pencil on his desk during tests, a rhythm that calmed her nerves more than any revision ever had. That one small, silly habit now surfaced like a lifeline between past and present.

"Let's get a drink," Ethan suggested, his hand lightly resting on her elbow as he guided her toward the bar. Emma's heart fluttered at the warmth of his touch, as if they hadn't been strangers for a decade. She remembered the way his thumb used to trace small circles over her wrist when they held hands, a simple gesture that had once made her feel safe in a world that often wasn't. She fought to keep her composure, reminding herself that this was just a reunion, just an innocent catch-up with an old friend.

They found a quiet corner where the hum of chatter and music softened, giving them a semblance of privacy. Ethan ordered two glasses of wine, and for a few moments, they sipped in silence, the weight of unsaid words filling the space between them.

"So, how have you been?" he finally asked, his eyes holding that same warmth she remembered from their high school days.

Emma shrugged, glancing down at her glass as she traced her finger around the rim. "Oh, you know. Busy. Work keeps me on my toes, and... well, that's about it." She tried to laugh it off, but the words sounded hollow, even to her. "And you? Are you... are you married?" The question slipped out before she could stop herself, and she instantly regretted it.

He chuckled softly, shaking his head. "No, I'm not married. Came close once, but... it didn't work out." He gave her a wistful smile. "Funny how life never quite turns out the way we imagine, isn't it?"

Emma nodded, a lump forming in her throat. She had always thought she and Ethan would end up together, had imagined a life with him countless times before their paths diverged. But here they were, both a little older, a little wiser, yet undeniably connected.

"Why did you come?" he asked gently, his gaze steady and searching. "To the reunion, I mean."

She hesitated, her fingers fidgeting with the stem of her glass. "I wasn't going to come, honestly. I thought... well, I thought it might just be too hard." She hesitated, her fingers tightening slightly around the stem of her glass. A beat passed as she wrestled with the vulnerability that pressed at the edges of her composure. She looked up, meeting his eyes. "But then I realised that maybe I was afraid of seeing you. Or maybe I was afraid of not seeing you." The words tumbled out, surprising her with their honesty.

[12]

Ethan's face softened, and he leaned forward, his voice low and warm. "I thought about you, you know. Over the years. I'd see little things that reminded me of you—an old song on the radio, a book you once loved. And every time, I wondered if I'd made a mistake letting you go."

Her heart ached at his confession, a mixture of longing and regret settling between them. She noticed the way his eyes softened when he looked at her—the same expression he used to wear when he caught her staring across the library during study hall. The memory flickered through her like a breeze stirring old pages. She wanted to reach out, to close the distance, but uncertainty held her back.

"What if…" he began, his voice almost a whisper. "What if we didn't let go this time?"

The question hung in the air, trembling with possibility. Emma felt a surge of hope that was both exhilarating and terrifying. Could they truly pick up where they'd left off? Or had too much time and hurt passed between them?

"I don't know," she replied honestly, her voice barely audible. "But maybe… maybe we could try."

A slow smile spread across Ethan's face as he reached across the table to gently take her hand. His touch was warm, steady, grounding her in the present moment.

"Then let's start there," he said softly, his fingers intertwining with hers. A flicker of cautious hope bloomed in Emma's chest. Maybe this really was the beginning of something new—not a reprise, but a rebirth. "One step at a time."

Chapter 3: Old Memories, New Beginnings

The rain had subsided by the time Emma and Ethan left the reunion, and the city streets shimmered with reflections under the streetlights. As they walked side by side, a comfortable silence settled between them, each step bringing back memories of their long walks home after school, when life had seemed so simple—passing the corner bakery where they used to split a chocolate croissant, their hands brushing as they reached for the last bite, laughter echoing down quiet lanes.

"Do you remember that little café we used to go to?" Ethan asked, glancing sideways at her, a mischievous smile playing on his lips. "The one with the terrible coffee and mismatched chairs?"

Emma laughed, a lightness lifting something heavy within her. "I can't believe that place is still open," she replied, shaking her head. "We spent so many afternoons there, thinking we were so grown up."

"Let's go, for old times' sake," he suggested, his eyes bright with excitement.

She hesitated, glancing at her watch and aware of the late hour. But the hopeful look in his eyes, combined with the warmth she felt at his side, made her decision for her. "Why not?"

They strolled through the quiet streets, the city alive yet hushed, as if holding its breath just for them. When they reached the café, it was just as she remembered: dimly lit, cozy, and filled with the scent of stale coffee and cinnamon. They slid into one of the old booths by the window, the years melting away as they laughed over memories of teenage days filled with hope and endless plans—like the time they swore they'd move to Paris after graduation, live in a tiny flat with a view of the Seine, and write books in cafés all day. It had been ridiculous, romantic, and completely theirs.

"Remember the time we ditched class and hid out here, all because I wanted to avoid that history test?" Ethan asked, his eyes twinkling with mischief.

Emma laughed, nodding. "You bribed the waitress to keep our secret. I was so terrified we'd get caught. I think that was the only time I ever skipped a class."

Ethan grinned. "You were always the sensible one. That's what I loved about you. And still do," he added quietly, his gaze dropping for a moment, as if the admission had surprised him as much as it did her. Emma's breath caught slightly at the words, her pulse quickening. She hadn't expected something so honest, so soon, and it left her both disarmed and inexplicably hopeful. he added quietly, his gaze dropping for a moment, as if the admission had surprised him as much as it did her.

Emma's heart fluttered. This was more than nostalgia. It felt real, like a warmth spreading slowly, taking root in the present rather than in the past.

She took a deep breath, her fingers brushing over the rim of her coffee cup. "Ethan, I need to know... why didn't we stay in touch?"

He looked down, his expression turning serious. "I think I was scared," he admitted. "When we went off to university, I thought it was better to give us both space, to let you focus on your future without... any distractions."

"A distraction?" She raised an eyebrow, her voice light but with a hint of hurt. "I never saw you as a distraction, Ethan."

"I know," he replied, his voice softening as he reached across the table, his hand covering hers. "I thought I was doing the right thing, but I was wrong. Letting you go was one of the hardest things I've ever done. And I've regretted it more times than I can count."

Her chest tightened at his words. She wanted to be angry, to let him see the hurt she'd carried, but all she felt was the warmth of his hand over hers, the sincerity in his eyes, and a quiet, steady hope rising within her.

"Maybe it's not too late," she whispered, her voice barely audible. The words felt fragile on her lips, like a truth she hadn't dared to speak aloud until now. Her heart thudded in her chest, uncertain yet wide open.

Ethan looked at her, his eyes filled with the same longing she felt. "Emma," he said softly, "I don't want to make that mistake again. I know we're different people now, but maybe that's a good thing. Maybe we can make this work."

Emma felt a lump form in her throat as she nodded, blinking back the tears threatening to spill. "I'd like that."

They stayed at the café until closing, sharing stories and dreams they hadn't dared to voice in years. By the time they parted ways, Emma felt as if she'd been given a second chance—a glimpse of weekend mornings curled beside him with coffee and conversation, of laughter echoing in shared spaces, of a future built slowly, steadily, together. chance to find the happiness she thought she'd lost long ago.

As she walked home, a small smile tugged at her lips, a warmth filling her heart. She knew there would be challenges ahead, but for the first time in a long time, she felt ready to face them, with Ethan by her side.

Chapter 4: The Road to Forgiveness

Emma awoke the next morning feeling lighter than she had in years. The memories from the night before replayed like a gentle melody—Ethan's voice still echoing in her ears, the scent of rain-soaked pavement mingling with the warmth of his cologne, and the lingering feel of his hand clasping hers beneath the umbrella. Ethan's laughter, the warmth of his hand over hers, and the way he'd looked at her, as if she were still the girl he'd loved all those years ago.

She made her way to the kitchen, wrapped in the soft warmth of her robe, and poured herself a cup of tea. Her phone buzzed with a message, and her heart leapt when she saw Ethan's name on the screen.

Ethan: I had an amazing time last night. Can we meet again? Maybe this weekend? x

Emma's lips curved into a smile as she typed out her response.

Emma: I'd like that. Saturday? x

The days leading up to their date were filled with anticipation and a bit of nervousness. As much as she was excited to see him again, the shadow of past heartbreaks loomed. She had been disappointed in love before—most painfully, with Ethan himself, when silence and distance had taken the place of promises—and she wondered if her heart could truly take the risk again.

Saturday came quickly, and they met at a small Italian bistro near the Thames. Ethan was waiting at a corner table, a fresh bouquet of lilies—the ones she'd always loved—on the table beside him.

"I remembered," he said with a sheepish grin, handing her the flowers as she sat down.

"They're beautiful. Thank you," she replied, touched by the thoughtful gesture.

As they settled into dinner, conversation flowed easily between them. They talked about everything from their favourite films to their dream travel destinations. But as the evening wore on, a question lingered in Emma's mind, one she couldn't keep back any longer.

"Ethan," she said, her voice hesitant. "What happened after we stopped talking? Why didn't you ever try to reach out?"

Ethan's smile faded slightly as he looked down, his fingers tracing the rim of his glass. "After we went our separate ways, I thought about calling you a thousand times. I even dialed your number more than once. But I'd convinced myself that you were better off without me. I was afraid I'd hold you back."

Emma's heart ached at his words, but she remained silent, letting him continue. A flicker of their last goodbye rushed back—his unread message, her unanswered questions—and for a moment, she wasn't sure if she wanted to cry or simply breathe him in.

"I thought if I stayed out of your life, you'd move on, find someone who could give you everything I couldn't. I tried to move on too," he admitted, his voice thick with regret. "But no matter who I was with, it always came back to you."

Emma took a deep breath, absorbing his confession. She had wondered so many times if she hadn't been enough, if he'd simply grown tired of her. But hearing his reasons now, she felt both the weight of his fears and the sincerity of his regret.

"Ethan," she said softly, reaching out to place her hand over his. "All I ever wanted was you. And even when things got hard, I would've chosen you, every time. I wish you'd known that."

They sat in silence, the weight of unspoken forgiveness settling between them. Emma's fingers gently tightened around his, and Ethan exhaled softly, his shoulders lowering as though he'd finally set down a burden he'd carried for far too long. Ethan squeezed her hand, a hint of moisture in his eyes.

"Emma, I don't deserve a second chance. But if you'll give me one, I promise I won't let you down."

[21]

A shiver ran through her, a mix of hope and trepidation. She'd been hurt so many times before, by men who hadn't cared, by men who had left without a second thought. But looking into Ethan's eyes now, she felt something she hadn't felt in years: trust.

"You have a second chance," she replied quietly, her voice barely more than a whisper. "But I want us to take it slow. I don't want to rush into anything and end up hurt again."

Ethan nodded, his face softening with understanding. "Slow sounds perfect to me. I'm just grateful for the chance."

They finished dinner with lighter hearts, laughing over dessert and sharing stories of all the moments they'd missed in each other's lives. By the time they left the bistro, a gentle rain had started to fall, misting the air with a fresh, earthy scent.

Ethan pulled her close, sheltering her under his umbrella as they walked. They didn't need to say much; their hearts seemed to speak louder than words in the silence. And as they reached her doorstep, he paused, looking at her with a gentle, hopeful gaze.

"Goodnight, Emma," he said, his voice warm, laced with the promise of a future they might finally get to share.

"Goodnight, Ethan," she replied, her heart full, as she slipped inside, feeling like the broken pieces of her heart were finally coming together again. The soft scent of lilies lingered on her coat, and in the quiet of her hallway, she allowed herself to imagine what healing might look like—slow mornings, shared silences, and a love rebuilt, one careful step at a time.

Chapter 5: Past Shadows

The days following their dinner felt like a dream to Emma. The glow of candlelight still flickered in her memory, the echo of Ethan's laughter lingering like a favourite song replaying softly in her mind. She and Ethan fell into an easy rhythm, texting throughout the day and meeting for quiet walks along the river or cozy dinners in tucked-away restaurants. She felt a warmth and joy she hadn't known in years, a gentle hope that maybe—just maybe—this time would be different.

But as time went on, Emma couldn't help but notice small shadows lingering in her heart. She remembered the long silences after their last argument years ago, the way his absence had left an ache she'd tucked away but never truly healed. The joy was real, but so were the memories of the disappointments and heartbreaks that had marked her past. With Ethan's reappearance, she found herself wondering if she was truly ready to let her guard down completely.

One Sunday morning, as they walked through Hyde Park with cups of hot coffee warming their hands, Ethan paused and turned to her, his gaze thoughtful. "I was thinking," he began slowly, "about introducing you to my family again. They've been asking about you ever since I mentioned we'd reconnected."

Emma felt a pang of both excitement and trepidation. Meeting his family again felt like a significant step, one that would place her firmly back in his life. "Are you sure?" she asked, trying to keep her tone light. "It's only been a few weeks."

"I know," Ethan replied, giving her a reassuring smile. "But you're important to me, Emma. I don't want to hide that anymore."

His words made her heart swell with affection, yet she couldn't ignore the flicker of doubt that crept in. This had all happened so quickly, this feeling of stepping back into each other's lives as though no time had passed. While part of her was grateful for it, another part—a deeper, more cautious part—worried about whether they could truly move beyond their history.

The week passed, and Ethan arranged for her to come to his family's house for Sunday lunch. As she got ready that morning, Emma found herself lingering in front of the mirror, a bundle of nerves. She adjusted the delicate silver necklace at her throat, remembering how she'd worn it for a holiday dinner with Ethan's family years ago, back when everything had felt so simple and laughter had come easily between them, remembering how she'd worn it for a holiday dinner with Ethan's family years ago, back when everything had felt so simple.

When she arrived at Ethan's family home, she was greeted with warmth and familiarity, his mother embracing her as if no time had passed. The afternoon was filled with laughter, stories, and reminiscing about the "good old days" when she and Ethan were inseparable.

As the meal drew to a close, Ethan's mother took Emma aside, her eyes filled with kindness but also a hint of motherly caution.

"Emma," she began gently, reaching out to touch her hand. "I've always cared for you, and I know how much you meant to Ethan all those years ago. He was heartbroken when you drifted apart."

Emma felt a pang of guilt mixed with sadness, knowing how much pain their separation had caused. "I've always cared about him too," she replied softly. "I just... I needed time."

His mother nodded understandingly. "I understand, dear. But please, be gentle with him. He's been through a lot, and I can see how much he still cares for you. I just hope that if you're both stepping back into each other's lives, it's because you're truly ready."

Emma nodded, a lump forming in her throat. She had been prepared for this—a family's loving concern—but it still weighed on her heart. Ethan's family had always treated her as one of their own, and she didn't want to disappoint them or risk the connection they'd once shared. But in her own heart, doubts still lingered.

After lunch, as she and Ethan took a quiet walk through the garden, she voiced the thoughts she'd been keeping in the back of her mind.

"Ethan," she began, her voice hesitant, "I don't want to rush things. I don't want to make promises I can't keep, and I don't want either of us to end up hurt." Her voice trembled slightly, the words tasting of old wounds and fragile hope. Part of her feared saying too much, the other feared saying too little.

He turned to face her, his gaze steady and understanding. "Emma, I know you're scared. I am too. But I'm willing to take this one day at a time with you. We don't have to have it all figured out right now."

Relief washed over her, and she felt the tension in her chest ease slightly. "Thank you," she whispered. "I just... I want this to be different. I want it to last."

They stood there, wrapped in a gentle silence, each holding onto the fragile hope that somehow, they could move beyond the shadows of their past. And as the afternoon sun dipped below the horizon, casting a warm glow over the garden, Emma felt the faint stirrings of a quiet assurance. She imagined Sunday mornings spent in that very garden, their laughter blending with birdsong, hands entwined over steaming mugs of coffee—proof that healing wasn't just possible, it had already begun. She wasn't alone in this, and maybe—just maybe—they could find a way forward together.

Chapter 6: Opening Old Wounds

The following weeks saw Emma and Ethan building a careful, steady rhythm, yet Emma's heart still bore the scars of old wounds—like the silence that followed their first goodbye, and the rainy afternoon she waited by the phone for a call that never came. Each time Ethan pulled her close or whispered something tender, a part of her wondered how long it would last, haunted by the lingering shadows of the times they had drifted apart.

One evening, as they sat in Emma's cozy living room, curled up on the sofa with a glass of wine, she felt the urge to bring up the question she'd been avoiding. She knew it was risky, but the uncertainty gnawed at her, and she wanted clarity before she invested her whole heart. If this faltered again, she wasn't sure she could survive the kind of heartbreak that had once left her doubting everything—love, timing, even herself.

"Ethan," she began, her voice soft but steady, "there's something I need to know." She placed her wineglass on the coffee table, turning to face him fully.

He looked at her, sensing the seriousness in her tone. "Of course. What's on your mind?"

She took a deep breath, the words tumbling out before she could second-guess herself. She hesitated, her fingers twisting in her lap as a knot formed in her stomach. The question had lived in her heart for years, unspoken but never forgotten. "Why did you stay away all those years?? I know you said you thought it was better for both of us, but… was that really the only reason?"

Ethan's expression softened, and he reached for her hand, giving it a gentle squeeze. "Emma," he began slowly, "I won't lie. Part of me wanted to come back to you so many times, but I was struggling with my own fears and doubts. When we separated, I convinced myself that I couldn't give you the stability you deserved. I thought if I kept my distance, you'd find someone better suited for you."

Her heart tightened as he spoke, feeling both the sadness of his words and the sincerity behind them. But a small, nagging voice inside her couldn't help but push further—the same voice that had whispered doubt on lonely nights, reminding her of how easily love had slipped through her fingers once before.

"Did you… did you ever think about us, though?" she asked quietly, her voice barely a whisper. "Did you ever imagine that we might have had a second chance?"

Ethan's face grew serious, his gaze drifting to a distant point beyond her. "Emma, I thought about you every day. I thought about what could have been, what I'd lost. But I was afraid that if I reached out and you had moved on… I don't know if I could've handled that."

Emma felt a pang of sorrow and understanding, knowing he had battled his own regrets, just as she had. But even as he confessed his feelings, a small voice inside her still asked if she could trust him, if he truly meant to stay this time.

They sat in silence for a few moments, each absorbed in their own thoughts. Finally, Ethan turned to her, his eyes earnest. "Emma, I know I messed up by letting you go. I'll spend the rest of my life making up for it, if you'll let me."

A part of her softened at his words, but the weight of past disappointments held her back. She knew she needed to take things slow, to let her heart heal fully, but a question lingered in her mind—one that had troubled her for some time.

"Ethan," she said, her voice barely more than a whisper. "What if… what if this doesn't work out? What if we're not meant to be together after all?"

He looked at her, his gaze steady and understanding. "Emma, I can't promise that everything will be perfect. But I can promise that I'll be here, that I'll fight for us this time. I'm not the same person I was back then. I'm ready to commit, fully, to whatever the future holds for us."

She searched his face, seeing the sincerity in his eyes, and a small flicker of hope began to blossom within her. She knew the road ahead wouldn't be easy, but she was willing to give it a chance, the weight in her chest beginning to ease, like thawing ice under a timid spring sun. Hope, she realised, felt like breath returning after being held for far too long, to see if they could rebuild the love they'd once shared.

They spent the rest of the evening in quiet conversation, talking about their dreams, their fears, and the lessons they'd learned along the way. For the first time in years, Emma felt a sense of peace, as if the pieces of her life were finally beginning to fall into place.

As the night wore on, she found herself leaning into Ethan's embrace, feeling the warmth and comfort of his presence. She knew there would be challenges ahead, but for now, in this moment, she felt as if she was exactly where she was meant to be.

Chapter 7: Shadows of Doubt

Over the next few weeks, Emma and Ethan settled into an easy rhythm, sharing quiet dinners, weekend strolls, and the kind of heartfelt conversations she had missed for so long. Yet, despite the tenderness growing between them, Emma's old doubts lingered like shadows around the edges of her heart—especially the memory of that last phone call, when silence fell between them and he never called back. It had left a mark she struggled to forget, even now.

One Friday evening, they found themselves in a cozy jazz club downtown, a place Ethan had suggested to bring something new into their usual routines. The warm, dim lights and soft music created the perfect atmosphere for a night of laughter and shared memories. As they swayed to the music, Emma felt a rare peace settle within her—a brief pause from the worries that often crowded her mind.

But as the evening progressed, a familiar thought crept in—a voice she hadn't quite silenced. Was this simply a return to what once was? Was she seeing Ethan for who he was now, or was she clinging to a memory of the past, to the boy who once sketched her portrait in a notebook during study hall, promising that they'd never drift apart, hoping to recreate something they'd both lost?

As if sensing her change in mood, Ethan leaned closer, his voice soft. "What's on your mind?"

Emma hesitated, not wanting to dampen the evening, but she knew that honesty was the only way forward if they truly wanted a second chance. "Ethan," she began, choosing her words carefully, "do you ever worry that we're... I don't know, trying to recreate the past?"

He looked at her thoughtfully, his brow furrowing slightly. "Sometimes, yes," he admitted, his tone gentle. "But that doesn't mean we can't build something new. We're not the same people we were back then, Emma. And I don't want the same relationship we had. I want something better."

His words offered a small measure of reassurance, but the ache of old hurts remained, not quite healed. "It's just... hard," she said quietly, her voice barely audible above the music. "I want to believe we're different now, that we can make this work. But I also know how much it hurt to let you go the first time."

Ethan reached for her hand, his fingers warm and steady over hers. Emma's breath caught at the familiar touch—a simple gesture, yet it broke through her guarded thoughts like sunlight through a shuttered window. "I understand, Emma. And if I could take back the years we lost, I would. But I want to prove to you, every day, that I'm here for you—for us. I want us to take things slow, to build trust, because I know that's the only way this can last."

Emma's heart softened at his words, the sincerity in his gaze easing some of the tension she felt. She nodded, her grip on his hand tightening slightly. "I want that too," she murmured, her voice wavering with emotion. "I just need to learn how to trust again."

They stayed silent for a moment, each lost in thought. The jazz band started another slow tune, and without a word, Ethan guided her into a gentle sway, holding her close as they moved to the rhythm. Emma let herself lean into him, the warmth of his embrace bringing a fragile sense of peace.

Just as she felt herself relax, her phone vibrated in her purse. She pulled back slightly, glancing at the screen. It was a message from her best friend, Lucy.

Lucy: Hey, I know you're out, but I thought you'd want to know—saw Ethan with someone last night. Looked like a business dinner, but just thought I should let you know.

Emma's heart sank, a chill running through her. It could be nothing, she told herself. Ethan had mentioned his work was demanding, and he often met clients or associates for dinner. But the message stirred something fragile within her, a worry she had tried so hard to suppress. What if he hadn't changed? What if he still had the potential to hurt her, to make her feel like she was just another piece of his life that could be set aside?

Ethan noticed her expression shift, concern flickering in his eyes. "Is everything okay?"

Emma forced a smile, slipping her phone back into her purse. But Lucy's message echoed louder than the music—reminding her of a time when Ethan had failed to show up, offering no explanation, no apology. That same ache flickered beneath her ribs now, uninvited and unwelcome. "Yeah, just Lucy being… Lucy," she replied, her tone light. But she could feel the doubt creeping in, like an unwelcome guest intruding on the evening.

They continued their dance, but Emma's mind was far from the music. She tried to brush off the message, to convince herself that it meant nothing. But the fear of being hurt again lingered, casting a shadow over her heart.

When Ethan walked her to her door that night, he reached for her hand, pulling her close. "Emma, I meant what I said earlier. I want to build something real with you. But if you ever feel unsure, I need you to tell me. I don't want us to lose each other because of things left unsaid."

Emma nodded, the weight of his words heavy on her heart. "I know," she replied, her voice barely a whisper. "I'll try."

They shared a gentle kiss, a moment of warmth amid the doubts stirring within her. As she closed the door and leaned against it, she couldn't shake the unease. She wanted to trust him, to let herself believe that this time would be different. But as much as her heart yearned for that happy ending, the shadows of the past held her back, whispering fears she wasn't ready to face. She wrapped her arms around herself as the faint scent of his cologne lingered in the hallway—comforting, yet uncertain—like a promise half-remembered in a dream.

Chapter 8: The Seeds of Doubt

Emma couldn't shake the unease that had settled within her after Lucy's message. She tried to dismiss it, convincing herself it was nothing, but the seeds of doubt had already been planted, their roots spreading deeper with each passing day. She had come to a place of fragile hope with Ethan, built slowly after that quiet evening on the sofa when she had dared to trust again—but now, a familiar fear lingered, whispering that she might be making a mistake by letting him back into her life so easily.

Days passed, and while her time with Ethan was filled with laughter and warmth, she found herself holding back, her guard slipping back into place without her fully realising it. Little things that wouldn't have bothered her before—like the times he had to cancel plans or answered texts late—began to gnaw at her, tightening her chest with a nervous flutter and keeping her awake at night with restless thoughts, stirring up insecurities she thought she had left behind.

One evening, while she and Lucy were out for coffee, Emma finally confided her worries.

"Am I being paranoid?" she asked, staring into her coffee as if it might reveal answers. "I mean, he's been wonderful, really. But ever since you mentioned seeing him with someone, I can't stop wondering if he's keeping something from me."

Lucy placed a comforting hand over hers. "Emma, I didn't mean to worry you. I just thought you'd want to know. But you're the only one who really knows him now. Maybe just ask him about it directly. If he's serious about you, he'll understand."

Emma nodded, letting Lucy's words sink in. The thought of losing what she'd finally started to rebuild filled her with a quiet dread. She wasn't just afraid of being lied to—she was afraid of once again having to piece herself back together from the fragments of another false hope. She knew Lucy was right—if she wanted this relationship to work, she couldn't let her insecurities fester in silence. She needed to be open with Ethan, to trust that he would be honest with her. But the idea of confronting him made her stomach twist, and she couldn't shake the fear of what his reaction might reveal.

The following weekend, Emma and Ethan had planned a quiet evening together at her place. She'd decided it was the perfect opportunity to clear the air, to let him know about her concerns without sounding accusatory. Yet as the evening wore on, her resolve wavered. He was warm and attentive, and as they sat side by side on the sofa, he seemed completely at ease. She didn't want to ruin the moment, but her mind kept drifting back to that message.

After a while, Ethan noticed her distraction. His expression shifted from relaxed to concerned. "Emma, is everything okay? You've been a bit quiet tonight."

She took a deep breath, summoning the courage to address what had been troubling her. "There is something I wanted to ask you about," she began carefully. "It's silly, really, but... Lucy mentioned she saw you with someone a few days ago. She thought it might've been a business meeting, but... I just wanted to ask."

Ethan's eyebrows lifted slightly, his expression a mixture of surprise and amusement. "Oh, that. Yeah, it was a business meeting. I had dinner with a client from out of town." He paused, a soft smile crossing his face. "Emma, you can always ask me anything. I don't want you to feel like you can't trust me."

She felt a wave of relief, but something within her remained unsettled. She hesitated, then spoke again, her voice softer this time. "It's just... I've been hurt before, Ethan. And sometimes, I wonder if I'm letting old fears get in the way."

Ethan's face softened, and he reached for her hand, his grip firm and reassuring. "Emma, I know we have a history, and I know I wasn't there for you the way I should've been back then. But I'm here now, and I'm not going anywhere. I want us to move forward, together."

Her heart swelled at his words, and for a moment, she felt the last of her doubts slipping away. It was like watching storm clouds part after days of grey, the first sunlight breaking through and touching her skin with fragile warmth. She leaned into him, resting her head on his shoulder as they sat in comfortable silence, the warmth of his presence easing her worries. Maybe she could trust him—truly trust him. Maybe this time, it would be different.

As the night grew late, they shared quiet laughter and tender moments, and Emma found herself feeling hopeful once again. But as he left that evening, a part of her still wondered if she was holding on to something too tightly, if her heart was still too guarded to fully open up.

In the days that followed, Emma worked on letting go of her doubts, reminding herself of Ethan's reassurances and the kindness he'd shown her. She wanted to believe in the possibility of a fresh start, to let her heart be free from the weight of past hurts.

But one afternoon, as she was out for a walk, her phone buzzed with a message—from an unknown number.

Unknown: Thought you should know Ethan hasn't been entirely honest with you. People don't change overnight.

Emma's heart dropped, her fingers trembling as she read the message again. It was like hearing that voicemail years ago—the one that shattered her trust and left her

[40]

questioning everything she thought she knew. The same cold panic crept in now, curling around her ribs with paralysing familiarity. She knew she should ignore it, that it could be nothing more than a cruel attempt to sabotage her happiness. But the familiar ache of doubt resurfaced, twisting in her chest as old fears came rushing back.

For a long moment, she stood there, staring at the message, torn between the hope she'd started to build with Ethan and the wounds of her past that refused to heal. She wanted to trust him, to believe they could make this work. But the shadows of doubt were strong, and she knew that if she didn't confront this head-on, it would haunt her and their relationship.

She took a deep breath, steeling herself for the confrontation she knew would come. She wasn't sure if she was ready, but one thing was certain: she needed the truth, whatever it might be.

Chapter 9: Confronting the Truth

Emma paced her living room, the message from the unknown number glaring up at her from her phone. Her heart felt heavy, filled with the weight of suspicion and hope battling within her. She knew confronting Ethan was risky; if she misjudged him, she could hurt them both. She pictured the night he left without a word, the silence that echoed for weeks afterward—a silence she had filled with questions and self-blame. But if there was truth to the message, she needed to know now, before allowing herself to fall any further.

After a few moments of indecision, she dialed his number, her fingers trembling slightly as the phone rang. When he answered, his familiar voice was warm and cheerful, as if he hadn't a care in the world.

"Emma, hey! I was just thinking about you," he said.

She took a deep breath, trying to steady herself. "Hi, Ethan. Could we talk? There's... something I need to ask you."

The pause on the other end was brief but unmistakable. "Of course," he replied, his tone shifting. "Is everything alright?"

"I'm not sure," she admitted. "Can you come over?"

Within half an hour, Ethan was at her door, concern etched on his face. He took one look at her, then reached for her hands, his touch warm and grounding. "Emma, what's going on? You look like something's really bothering you."

She swallowed, pulling her hands back to cross her arms protectively over her chest. "I got a message," she began slowly. "It was from an unknown number. They said... they said you haven't been honest with me."

Ethan's expression shifted from concern to confusion, his brow furrowing. "Emma, I don't understand. A message from an unknown number? What did it say, exactly?"

"They said you can't be trusted, that people don't change overnight," she said, her voice barely a whisper. Emma's throat tightened as the words left her. A memory surfaced—her friend warning her years ago not to fall so fast, not to believe in promises that came too easily. That ache returned now, raw and sharp in her chest," she said, her voice barely a whisper. "And I know it sounds ridiculous, but after everything I've been through... I just can't ignore it. I needed to hear the truth from you, Ethan. Are you hiding anything from me?"

He took a deep breath, his gaze steady as he looked into her eyes. "Emma, I've been nothing but honest with you. I told you everything about my past and why I stayed away. I'm here now because I want this—us—to work."

His words were calm and sincere, but she felt the shadow of doubt lingering, clinging to her like a fog. "But Ethan... why would someone send that message? Why would someone want to warn me about you?"

He shook his head slowly, his gaze pained. "I don't know. Maybe it's someone who doesn't want us to be happy. Maybe it's just a cruel prank. I don't know who would do this, but Emma, you have to trust me."

She wanted to believe him; she wanted to let go of the doubts, but they clenched in her stomach like a coiled spring, her hands tightening unconsciously at her sides as if bracing for another fall and fears that clung to her heart. But a voice in the back of her mind, one born from years of heartbreak and disappointment, kept urging her to be cautious. "I do want to trust you," she whispered, her voice wavering. "But I'm scared. I'm scared of being hurt again, of opening up just to be left alone."

Ethan took a step closer, his expression softening. "Emma, I know you've been hurt, and I know I'm partly to blame for that. But I'm here now, and I'm not going anywhere. Whatever you need to feel safe, I'm willing to do it."

She felt tears prick at her eyes, her heart aching with the tension between her hope and her fear. "What if I can't ever get past this?" she asked, her voice barely more than a whisper.

He reached out, brushing a tear from her cheek. "Then I'll be here every step of the way. Emma, I don't want you to do this alone. Let me prove to you that I'm here for the long haul."

His words wrapped around her like a gentle embrace, and she felt the first flickers of trust begin to resurface—tentative but real. Maybe this was her chance, she thought—a chance to let go of the walls she had built and open herself to the possibility of love once again.

They stood there, locked in a quiet moment of understanding, as if past wounds and present fears had finally found a space to heal. She reached for his hand, entwining her fingers with his, feeling the warmth of his steady presence grounding her.

"Alright," she murmured, her voice steady. "Let's move forward... together."

Ethan's face softened, a small, hopeful smile touching his lips. "That's all I want, Emma."

As he pulled her into an embrace, Emma felt a quiet sense of peace settling within her—a fragile hope that maybe, just maybe, they could find a way to build a future free from the shadows of their past. But she knew that trust was something they would have to work at, every day, with patience and understanding. And for the first time, she felt ready to try.

Chapter 10: New Beginnings, Old Wounds

For the next few weeks, Emma found herself settling into a quiet contentment she hadn't felt in years. Ethan had become her constant companion, showing her in small, thoughtful ways that he was there for her, that he genuinely wanted a fresh start. They took things slowly, as she'd requested, and each day, her trust in him grew, bit by bit.

But the shadows of doubt didn't vanish completely. Occasionally, Emma would catch herself questioning small things—an unreturned text, a late night at the office, a missed call. Each time, she forced herself to remember Ethan's reassurances and the commitment they had both made to move forward. Still, a part of her found it hard to let go entirely.

One evening, as they walked hand in hand through the park, Ethan stopped, looking at her with a nervous but hopeful expression. "Emma, I was thinking…" he began, glancing at the ground before meeting her gaze. "Maybe it's time we took the next step. I'd love for you to meet my close friends. We're getting together this Friday. Nothing big, just a casual dinner. I'd really like you to be there."

Emma hesitated, feeling both excitement and apprehension. Meeting his friends felt like a significant step, a sign that he wanted her to be part of every aspect of his life. "I'd like that," she replied, offering him a soft smile. "I'd love to meet them."

Friday came quickly, and Emma found herself standing outside Ethan's friend Mark's house, her heart racing with nerves. She had dressed carefully, choosing a dress that was casual yet elegant, wanting to make a good impression. As they walked in, she was greeted warmly by Mark and his wife, who immediately put her at ease with their friendly smiles and easy conversation.

Throughout the evening, Emma observed the dynamic between Ethan and his friends, feeling a sense of belonging as they shared stories, laughed, and teased one another. She began to feel like she was stepping into Ethan's world, learning about the people who had been part of his life during the years they'd spent apart.

As the evening progressed, however, she couldn't help but notice a slight tension lingering in the air. Ethan's friend Claire seemed to watch her closely, her smile polite but reserved. Several times, Emma caught Claire's gaze on her—a curious look that she couldn't quite interpret. Emma tried to ignore it, but a feeling of unease began to creep in, unsettling her.

Later, as they all gathered around the table for dessert, Claire leaned forward, her eyes fixed on Emma. "So, Emma," she began, her tone casual but with an edge that made Emma's heart skip a beat. "Ethan's told us so much about you. You two must have a lot of... history, considering you're giving things a second try."

Emma felt a flush rise to her cheeks, uncertain of how to respond. She forced a smile, trying to keep her tone light. "Yes, we've known each other for a long time. I suppose you could say we both needed a bit of time to find our way back to each other."

Claire's smile was polite, but something in her eyes suggested she had more to say. "It's just... Ethan's been through a lot. We were there for him when things didn't work out the first time. It's good to see him happy again, but I think we're all just a bit... protective."

The words were gentle, but Emma felt the weight of them settle heavily in her chest. She understood that Claire was a close friend, someone who had likely seen Ethan at his lowest. But a flicker of insecurity ignited within her, a worry that maybe she wasn't entirely welcome—that perhaps Ethan's friends still saw her as the one who had let him go.

Ethan, sensing the tension, reached over and placed a reassuring hand on her shoulder. "Claire," he said, his tone gentle but firm. "Emma and I both made mistakes, but we're here now, and that's what matters."

Claire nodded, her expression softening slightly. "Of course. I didn't mean to pry. I just want you to be sure, Ethan."

The rest of the evening passed without incident, but as they drove home, Emma couldn't shake the unease that had settled within her. Ethan had defended her, but Claire's words lingered in her mind, fueling the insecurities she had been working so hard to overcome.

"I'm sorry about Claire," Ethan said softly, glancing at her as he drove. "She can be a bit… blunt. But she means well."

Emma nodded, forcing a smile. "It's alright. I understand. She's looking out for you."

He reached for her hand, giving it a gentle squeeze. "You don't have to worry about what she thinks, Emma. I'm here because I want to be, because I believe in us."

She nodded again, comforted by his words, but a small part of her couldn't shake the doubt that had crept in. As much as she wanted to let herself believe in the future they were building, the fear of history repeating itself lingered, casting a shadow over her heart.

That night, as she lay in bed, she found herself thinking about Claire's words, about the lingering feeling that maybe, just maybe, she wasn't ready to fully trust. The weight of the unknown, the unpredictability of love, loomed over her, challenging her to either let go of her fears or risk letting them tear her and Ethan apart once again.

[49]

And as sleep finally claimed her, she knew that sooner or later, she would have to confront these insecurities, to find a way to silence the doubts that threatened to unravel everything she had worked so hard to rebuild.

Chapter 11: Embracing the Present

The morning sun streamed through the curtains, casting a warm glow across Emma's bedroom. She stirred awake, the remnants of a restless sleep clinging to her like a heavy fog. A flicker of an unfinished dream still lingered—Ethan's face half-turned away, the sound of his voice muffled in the distance—leaving her chest tight with unspoken questions. The encounter with Claire lingered in her mind, replaying in fragments that fueled her lingering doubts. She knew she couldn't continue like this—caught between hope and fear, past and present.

Determined to clear her head, Emma decided to spend the day focusing on herself. She pulled on comfortable clothes and headed to her favourite café, a quaint little spot nestled between a bookstore and a flower shop. The aroma of freshly brewed coffee and baked pastries enveloped her as she settled into a corner seat by the window.

As she sipped her latte, Emma pulled out a notebook—a habit she'd picked up to sort through her thoughts. She began jotting down everything that weighed on her: her fears of getting hurt again, the uncertainty about Ethan's feelings, and the nagging insecurities that seemed to shadow her every step.

Lost in her writing, she didn't notice when someone approached her table until a familiar voice broke through her reverie.

"Mind if I join you?"

She looked up to see Lucy standing there, a concerned smile on her face. "Lucy! What are you doing here?"

"I was just passing by and saw you through the window," Lucy replied, holding up a to-go cup. "Thought I'd say hi. You seemed deep in thought."

Emma gestured to the seat across from her. "Please, sit. I could use the company."

Lucy settled in, her gaze falling on the open notebook. "Writing a novel?" she teased gently.

Emma sighed, closing the notebook. "Just trying to make sense of things."

"Want to talk about it?"

Emma hesitated, then nodded. "I met Ethan's friends last night. For the most part, it was great, but one of them, Claire, made a few comments that stirred up old insecurities."

Lucy raised an eyebrow. "What did she say?"

"She hinted that they were protective of Ethan because of our past. It felt like she was warning me not to hurt him again. It brought back all my doubts about whether I'm good enough or if I can make this work. I remembered that dinner party with Daniel, how his mother's quiet disapproval had lingered in every glance, making me question whether I belonged at all. That same feeling crept in again, uninvited and sharp."

Lucy reached across the table, squeezing Emma's hand. "Emma, you are more than good enough. You've been through so much, and it's natural to have doubts. But don't let someone else's opinion derail your happiness."

"I know," Emma replied softly. "But it's not just Claire. It's me. I keep waiting for the other shoe to drop, for something to go wrong. I don't want to sabotage this, but I'm afraid I might."

Lucy gave her a sympathetic look. "Have you talked to Ethan about how you're feeling?"

"Not yet. I don't want to seem insecure or needy."

"Emma," Lucy said gently, "communication is key. Ethan can't support you if he doesn't know what's going on. Maybe it's time to let him in a little more."

Emma considered her friend's advice, a sense of resolve beginning to form. "You're right. I need to be honest with him."

Later that afternoon, Emma called Ethan. The echo of Lucy's words and the clarity from her morning reflections gave her a quiet strength. She realised that hiding her fears was more damaging than sharing them—and that reaching out was the first step to healing. "Hey, do you have time to meet up today?" she asked.

"Absolutely," he replied without hesitation. "Is everything okay?"

"I just want to talk. How about we meet at the park?"

"Sounds perfect. I'll see you in an hour."

As Emma waited on a bench beneath the shade of an old oak tree, she watched children playing and couples strolling hand in hand. A gentle breeze rustled the leaves above, and she took a deep breath, letting the calmness of the surroundings steady her nerves.

Ethan arrived, his face lighting up when he saw her. "Hey," he said warmly, taking a seat beside her. "You had me a little worried."

She offered a small smile. "Sorry, I didn't mean to worry you. I just needed to sort through some things."

He nodded, his eyes attentive. "I'm all ears."

Emma took a moment to gather her thoughts. "I wanted to talk about last night. Meeting your friends was...

enlightening. For the most part, I felt welcomed, but Claire's comments brought up some old insecurities."

Ethan sighed softly. "I was afraid of that. Claire can be a bit protective. She's seen me at my worst, and I think she worries."

"I understand that," Emma said. "But it made me realise that I still have a lot of fears—about us, about whether I can fully trust this. I don't want to keep doubting, but it's hard."

He reached for her hand, his touch gentle. "Emma, I appreciate your honesty. I want you to know that it's okay to have these feelings. I have my own fears, too. But I believe that we can work through them together."

She looked into his eyes, finding reassurance in his steady gaze. "I don't want to let my past dictate our future. I want to be able to trust you completely, to give us a real chance."

Ethan squeezed her hand lightly. "Then let's make a promise—to be open with each other, even when it's hard. No more holding back."

She nodded, a weight lifting from her shoulders. "Agreed. No more holding back."

They sat in comfortable silence for a moment, the sounds of the park filling the air around them. Emma felt a newfound sense of peace, as if voicing her fears had diminished their power over her.

"There's something I've been wanting to show you," Ethan said suddenly, a hint of excitement in his voice.

"Oh? What's that?"

He stood, pulling her up with him. "It's a surprise. Come on."

They walked a short distance to a small art gallery tucked away on a quiet street. Inside, the walls were adorned with various paintings and photographs, each telling its own story. Ethan led her to a section showcasing local artists.

"I've been working with the gallery owner to feature some new talent," he explained.

Emma's eyes widened as she took in a series of photographs depicting everyday scenes in striking detail. "These are incredible."

Ethan smiled. "I thought you might appreciate them. And there's another reason I brought you here."

He guided her to a particular photograph—a candid shot of a woman standing at a café window, her expression thoughtful as she gazed outside. Emma gasped softly as she realised the woman was herself. For a moment, the world around her fell away, and she saw herself not through her own insecurities, but through Ethan's lens—calm, present, and worthy of being noticed. It was like discovering a part of herself she hadn't known was missing.

"When did you take this?" she asked, turning to him in surprise.

"About a month ago," he admitted sheepishly. "I was passing by and saw you writing in your notebook. You looked so peaceful, and I couldn't resist capturing the moment."

"I can't believe you did this," she said, her heart swelling.

"I wanted to show you how I see you," Ethan said softly. "Strong, contemplative, and incredibly inspiring."

Tears welled in her eyes, but this time they were tears of joy. "Ethan, this is... I don't know what to say."

"You don't have to say anything," he replied, taking her hands in his. "I care about you, Emma. More than words can express."

She smiled through her tears, a warmth spreading through her. "I care about you too. And I think I'm finally ready to let go of the past."

He pulled her into a gentle embrace, holding her close as the soft hum of the gallery surrounded them. In that

[57]

moment, Emma felt the last of her reservations fade away, replaced by a quiet certainty that she was exactly where she was meant to be.

As they left the gallery hand in hand, Emma knew that the road ahead wouldn't always be easy. Yet as she stepped into the golden light of the setting sun, the warmth on her skin felt like a quiet promise—of healing, of hope, and of love that could grow even through the cracks. But with openness, honesty, and a shared commitment to their future, she felt hopeful that they could face whatever challenges came their way— together.

Chapter 12: Tested by Time

The days following their visit to the gallery felt like a turning point for Emma. For the first time, she felt the weight of her past fears lifting, replaced by a quiet confidence. That morning, she'd sent the first message, unprompted, asking Ethan about his day—a small act, but one that once would have terrified her. Now, it felt like reclaiming her own voice in her relationship with Ethan. They continued spending time together, creating new memories and deepening the bond they'd worked so hard to rebuild.

One evening, as they relaxed in her living room, sharing stories and laughter over cups of tea, Ethan's phone buzzed. He glanced at the screen, and his expression shifted slightly as he read the message.

"Is everything okay?" Emma asked, sensing his distraction.

Ethan nodded, but there was a hint of tension in his voice. "It's work. I might need to go out of town for a few weeks. One of our projects hit a snag, and they're sending a team to sort it out."

Emma's heart sank a little. She knew that long-distance had been part of what strained them in the past. "How long would you be gone?"

"Three weeks, maybe four," he replied, reaching for her hand. "But I'll keep in touch every day. We'll make it work."

She nodded, trying to keep her own insecurities in check, remembering how distant he had become the last time work pulled him away—how she'd waited for texts that never came and felt the slow erosion of trust creep in with every unanswered silence. She wanted to believe in the strength of their relationship, but the thought of him being so far away stirred up old anxieties.

The next day, Emma helped him pack, keeping up a cheerful façade as they folded clothes and organized his travel essentials. They laughed, joked, and tried to keep things light, but a part of her couldn't shake the worry gnawing at her heart.

When it was finally time for him to leave, he pulled her into a long, warm embrace. "Emma, I know this isn't ideal, but it's only temporary. I'll be back before you know it."

She forced a smile, her voice steady but soft. "I know. I just… I'm going to miss you."

He kissed her forehead, holding her close. "I'll miss you too. But remember, this is just a small step in our journey. We'll get through it together."

With one last lingering kiss, he left, leaving Emma standing in the doorway, watching as he disappeared down the street. She felt a pang of sadness but reminded herself that they had come this far, and she wouldn't let her insecurities hold her back now.

Over the following days, they kept in touch through phone calls and texts, sharing moments of their days and laughing over video calls. But as the weeks passed, the distance began to feel more tangible—like the empty space beside her on the couch or the silence that greeted her each morning where his voice used to be—and Emma found herself struggling to stay positive.

One evening, as she was scrolling through her messages, a familiar feeling of doubt crept in. Ethan had been busier than usual, his texts shorter and his calls less frequent. She tried to push the worries aside, reminding herself of his reassurances, but the sense of distance felt overwhelming.

To distract herself, Emma decided to meet Lucy for dinner. As they chatted over pasta and wine, Lucy noticed Emma's subdued mood.

"You're missing him, aren't you?" Lucy asked gently, a knowing smile on her face.

Emma sighed, stirring her pasta absently. "I thought I'd be fine with the distance, but it's harder than I expected. I keep worrying, wondering if we're going to be okay."

Lucy reached across the table, giving her hand a reassuring squeeze. "Emma, you've come so far. Don't let fear steal this happiness from you. He's committed to you, and he'll be back soon."

Emma smiled, grateful for her friend's support. But as she lay in bed that night, her phone silent beside her, the doubts continued to linger. She hadn't heard from Ethan all day, and while she knew he was busy, a small part of her couldn't help but wonder if the distance was beginning to affect him too.

The following evening, Emma finally received a text from Ethan.

Ethan: Hey, sorry for being quiet. Things have been hectic. I'll call tomorrow—promise.

Relief washed over her, but she couldn't shake the feeling of isolation. It crept into her evenings like a fog, making her apartment feel colder, her dinner table emptier. Even music, once comforting, now echoed with a hollow edge that reminded her of the silence he left behind. that had begun to settle within her. She wanted to trust him fully, but the lack of communication made it hard to silence her doubts.

As the days passed, she began to fill her time with activities, immersing herself in work, meeting friends, and even picking up an art class to keep her mind occupied. But Ethan's absence weighed on her, a constant reminder of how fragile trust could feel when separated by miles.

One night, as she was about to fall asleep, her phone lit up with an incoming call. She answered, relief flooding her as she heard Ethan's voice.

"Hey, stranger," she teased lightly, masking her worry.

"Hey," he replied, his tone weary but affectionate. "I'm sorry for being so out of touch. Things have been intense here, but I didn't want you to think I'd forgotten about you."

"I know you're busy," she replied softly. "But I miss you, Ethan. More than I thought I would."

He sighed, and she could sense the exhaustion in his voice. "I miss you too. Just a few more days, and I'll be back. I promise, we'll make up for lost time."

They talked for a while longer, sharing small details of their days, and for the first time in weeks, Emma felt a sense of peace return. The call reminded her of why she had fought so hard to rebuild this relationship and why she was willing to wait.

Finally, the day of his return arrived, and Emma found herself anxiously waiting at the airport, her heart racing as she scanned the arrivals for a glimpse of him. When she finally saw him walking towards her, tired but smiling, she felt a surge of relief and joy that washed away the doubts she'd carried for weeks.

Ethan pulled her into his arms, holding her tightly as if he never wanted to let go. "I missed you so much," he murmured, pressing a soft kiss to her forehead.

"I missed you too," she replied, her voice thick with emotion. "I didn't realise how hard it would be, but... I'm so glad you're here."

They spent the rest of the day together, catching up and sharing stories from their time apart. And as they sat together in the quiet of her apartment that evening, Emma felt a renewed sense of certainty in her heart.

"Ethan," she began, looking at him with a newfound confidence. "I think I finally understand. Love isn't just about the happy moments. It's the way we held on through the silences, the missed calls, and the doubt. It's about choosing each other even when the path wasn't clear. It's about choosing to stay, to hold on, even when it's hard."

He nodded, his eyes filled with warmth. "Exactly. I know we'll face challenges, but I'm here for all of it, Emma. Every single moment."

They sat in comfortable silence, each wrapped in their own thoughts, yet bound by an unspoken understanding. For the first time, Emma felt as if she was truly ready to embrace their future, to hold on to the love they had rebuilt and to trust in the journey ahead.

As the evening faded into night, she knew that their love had been tested, but it had emerged stronger, forged by time, distance, and a commitment that ran deeper than any past hurt. And with Ethan by her side, she felt ready to face whatever lay ahead.

Chapter 13: Facing the Future

Emma and Ethan slipped into a rhythm over the weeks following his return, sharing slow Sunday mornings over coffee and crossword puzzles, taking evening walks where their fingers found each other without thought, and laughing at inside jokes that belonged only to them, settling into a warmth and ease that made Emma feel they were finally building something lasting. The once-frequent doubts she'd carried began to fade, replaced by a steady trust and quiet joy that filled her days. She hadn't felt this kind of contentment in years, and she found herself imagining a future with him—one filled with shared moments, laughter, and love.

One Saturday afternoon, as they wandered through an open-air market hand in hand, Ethan turned to her with a thoughtful look. "Emma," he began, his voice hesitant, "I wanted to talk to you about something."

Her heart skipped a beat, noticing the serious expression in his eyes. "Of course. What is it?"

He paused, running a hand through his hair as if searching for the right words. "There's an opportunity at work—a promotion, actually. It would mean more responsibility, but there's a catch."

She raised an eyebrow, intrigued but cautious. "What kind of catch?"

Ethan looked away briefly, his gaze drifting over the market stalls. "I'd have to relocate. It's a position in New York."

The words hit her like a sudden gust of wind, unexpected and unsettling. She felt her heart sink, a mixture of emotions swirling within her—pride for his success, fear of losing the closeness they'd worked so hard to build, and uncertainty about what this would mean for their future.

"New York?" she repeated, trying to keep her voice steady. The word conjured a memory of Ethan once nearly taking a job in Paris during their university days—how it had unravelled them slowly, across time zones and unread messages. Her heart thumped with a fear she thought she'd outgrown. "That's... a big change."

He nodded, his expression sombre. "I know. And I wouldn't make any decisions without talking to you first. You're a huge part of my life, Emma. I don't want to lose what we've built."

They walked in silence for a few moments, the vibrant energy of the market a stark contrast to the weight of their conversation. Emma felt a tightness in her chest as she tried to process the idea of Ethan living thousands of miles away. She had grown used to his presence, to the comfort of knowing he was just a call or a short drive away.

"What would it mean for us?" she asked softly, her voice filled with uncertainty. "Long-distance again?"

He took a deep breath, turning to face her fully. "That depends on what we both want, Emma. I'd be lying if I said I didn't want you to come with me. But I also know you have a life here, friends, a career. I don't want to put any pressure on you."

Emma felt the weight of his words, the unspoken question lingering between them. Moving to New York was a huge step—one that would change everything about her life. And while she loved Ethan, the idea of uprooting herself from her home and career felt overwhelming.

"Do you really want this job, Ethan?" she asked, needing to understand his heart.

He hesitated, then nodded. "I do. It's a chance to grow, to take on new challenges. But if it means losing you... I'm willing to stay here."

The sincerity in his voice touched her, but it also made her feel the importance of the decision they were facing. She knew she couldn't ask him to pass up an opportunity he cared about, yet the thought of moving felt daunting.

"Maybe we don't have to decide right now," she suggested, a flicker of hope in her voice. "We can take some time, think it over. It doesn't have to be all or nothing."

Ethan's face softened, and he reached for her hand, giving it a reassuring squeeze. "I'd like that. Whatever happens, I don't want to lose you, Emma."

They spent the rest of the afternoon in quiet companionship, both lost in their thoughts yet bound by a shared understanding. They continued to enjoy the market, browsing through stalls of handmade jewellery and fragrant candles, finding comfort in the familiarity of each other's presence.

But as the days passed, Emma couldn't shake the sense of uncertainty that had settled within her. She knew that Ethan's opportunity was important, and part of her wanted to support him fully, to take a leap of faith and imagine a life together in a new city. Yet another part of her felt rooted here, in the life she had built, the friendships she cherished, and the career she had worked so hard to establish.

One evening, as she sat with Lucy over a cup of tea, she confided her fears.

"I just don't know if I'm ready for such a big change," Emma admitted, stirring her tea absently. "I love Ethan, but the idea of moving across the world… it feels like I'd be leaving behind a part of myself."

Lucy nodded, her expression sympathetic. "It's a huge decision, Emma. But remember, this is your life too. You don't have to sacrifice everything for someone else's dreams."

Emma took a deep breath, absorbing her friend's words. Somewhere beneath her worry, a quiet clarity began to form—she didn't want to lose herself again. She had worked too hard to become the woman she was now: steady, whole, and brave enough to speak her truth. "I want to support him. I just don't know if I can give up everything here. And if I don't go… I'm afraid of what that might mean for us."

Lucy reached across the table, giving her hand a comforting squeeze. "Emma, whatever you decide, it has to be something you can live with. Love is important, but so is staying true to yourself. Maybe it's a question of finding a balance that works for both of you."

Emma spent the following days reflecting on Lucy's advice, grappling with the conflicting desires in her heart. She wanted a future with Ethan, but she also knew she couldn't give up everything she valued without feeling a sense of loss. After much thought, she realised that the only way forward was through open and honest communication.

A few days later, she invited Ethan over, ready to have the conversation she'd been avoiding. Her palms were clammy as she arranged the cushions on the sofa for the third time, her heart thudding with a quiet urgency. Every creak of the floorboards made her glance toward the door, wondering if she was prepared to say the things she'd rehearsed in her head a hundred times. As they sat together in her living room, she took a deep breath, steadying herself.

"Ethan," she began, her voice calm but resolute. "I've been thinking about New York, and… I don't know if I'm ready to move just yet. My life is here, and it's hard for me to imagine leaving it all behind."

Ethan nodded, his expression understanding. "I get it, Emma. I don't want to force you into anything. This is a big decision for both of us."

She reached for his hand, her gaze steady. "But I also don't want to lose you. Maybe… maybe we can find a way to make it work. Maybe we try long-distance again, just for a while, and see where it takes us."

He smiled, relief evident in his eyes. "Emma, that sounds perfect. I don't need all the answers right now. I just need to know that you're with me, no matter where we are."

They shared a quiet embrace, the uncertainty of the future still looming but tempered by a sense of commitment. For the first time, Emma felt at peace with the idea of taking things one step at a time, allowing their love the space to grow naturally.

As they held each other, she realised that love didn't always require drastic sacrifices. Sometimes it looked like two people choosing to stay in the same moment, wrapped in each other's arms, while the rest of the world waited outside their embrace. Sometimes, it was enough to be present, to face each challenge with patience and understanding. And in that moment, she knew that no

[71]

matter where life took them, she and Ethan would find a way to make it work—together.

Chapter 14: Learning to Let Go

The first weeks after Ethan's departure felt like a strange, empty silence in Emma's life. She had grown so used to his presence, his laughter filling her apartment, and his reassuring hand in hers. Now, each evening felt like an echo, reminding her of the distance between them. But they both knew this was the best path forward—for now. Emma told herself that space might give them clarity, that loving each other from afar could prove the strength of their bond rather than diminish it.

Their days followed a new routine. They texted each morning, exchanging cheerful greetings and updates on their plans for the day. At night, they made time for long video calls, sharing everything from mundane daily details to deeper conversations about their future. While it wasn't the same as having him beside her, Emma felt grateful for the technology that kept them connected.

One evening, as they talked over a video call, Ethan's face was alight with excitement. "You'll never guess what happened today!" he said, his eyes gleaming.

Emma smiled, leaning closer to her screen. "Tell me everything."

"We closed a huge deal," he explained, practically glowing. "Our team had been working on it for weeks, and today we finally got the green light. I haven't felt this exhilarated at work in ages."

Emma felt a swell of pride but also a slight pang of longing. She wished she could be there to celebrate with him, to toast his success in person. "That's amazing, Ethan. I'm so proud of you."

He beamed at her, his happiness infectious. "I owe a lot of it to you, you know. Your encouragement… it means everything."

The call continued, and they talked about his work and her latest projects. Yet, as the conversation wound down and she bid him goodnight, Emma felt a lingering emptiness—the kind that settled low in her chest, making her arms feel suddenly too heavy, as though the warmth of his voice had vanished too quickly and left the air around her cold ache of missing him more than she could put into words.

In the weeks that followed, Emma tried to fill her time with activities that brought her joy. She joined a book club, signed up for cooking classes, and even began volunteering at a local animal shelter. These moments of fulfillment were precious, and she found herself rediscovering passions she had set aside while focusing on her relationship.

But even with her busy schedule, there were moments when the loneliness crept in. One Saturday night, she attended a friend's engagement party. Watching the happy couple beam at each other, she felt a pang of envy. She remembered a night not long before Ethan left, when they had danced in her living room to a slow, crackling song on the radio, their laughter echoing in the dim light. That memory made the absence sharper, the space beside her more hollow. She knew her relationship with Ethan was strong, but the reality of their separation sometimes left her feeling adrift.

As she sat alone at her table, scrolling through photos of herself and Ethan, Lucy appeared, taking a seat beside her with a warm smile. "Hey, are you okay?" she asked, her tone gentle.

Emma forced a smile, slipping her phone back into her bag. "Yeah, just… missing him, I guess."

Lucy nodded knowingly. "Long-distance is tough. But you're one of the strongest people I know. If anyone can make it work, it's you two."

Emma sighed, fiddling with her drink. "I just feel like I'm in limbo. I love him, but it's hard to feel connected when he's so far away."

Lucy squeezed her shoulder. "You're doing great, Emma. Just take it one day at a time. If this is meant to be, you'll both find a way."

Later that night, as she lay in bed, Emma thought about Lucy's words. She realised that part of her struggle was learning to let go—to loosen her grip on the illusion of

[75]

control, like releasing a paper lantern into the night sky and trusting it would rise where it was meant to go, release her grip on the things she couldn't control and to trust in the strength of her love for Ethan. She didn't need to have everything figured out; she just needed to have faith in their journey.

A few days later, Ethan surprised her with a bouquet of lilies delivered to her office. Along with the flowers was a handwritten note:

"Emma, I know this distance is hard, but I promise we're one step closer to our future. I love you more than words can say. Yours, Ethan."

The gesture brought a smile to her face, filling her with a renewed sense of hope. She felt his love even across the miles, a reminder that while the separation was challenging, they were both committed to making it work.

Over the coming weeks, Emma found herself growing more accustomed to their new reality. She learned to find joy in her independence, embracing the moments of solitude as opportunities for growth. Each time she saw Ethan's name light up on her phone, she felt a surge of warmth and excitement—a reminder of the love they shared and the future they were building together.

One evening, as they talked over the phone, Ethan brought up a topic that had been on both their minds.

"Emma," he began, his voice hesitant, "I've been thinking a lot about our future. About how long we're going to keep doing this—being apart, I mean."

Emma's heart raced, a mixture of excitement and apprehension swirling within her. "I've been thinking about it too."

There was a pause, and she could sense the weight of his words even over the distance. "I don't want to pressure you, but... do you think you'd ever consider moving here?"

The question hung in the air, heavy with possibilities. She had known this conversation was coming, but now that it was here, she felt a surge of uncertainty. She loved her life in her city, her friends, her work—but she also knew how much she loved Ethan, how much he meant to her.

"I don't know," she admitted softly. "Part of me wants to, but part of me... is afraid of what I'd be giving up."

Ethan's voice was gentle, understanding. "I get it, Emma. And I don't want you to feel like you have to make a decision right now. I just needed you to know that whatever you decide, I'm here. And I'll wait as long as it takes."

Her heart swelled with gratitude and love for him, for the patience and kindness he showed her even in the face of uncertainty. "Thank you, Ethan. I just need a bit more time."

As they ended the call, Emma lay in bed, staring at the ceiling as a mix of emotions washed over her. She knew that sooner or later, a decision would need to be made. It hovered before her like a fork in a quiet road, waiting patiently, bathed in the golden haze of a future still unfolding. But for now, she resolved to take it one day at a time, to savour the love they shared and trust that they would find their way.

That weekend, she booked a ticket to visit him in New York, excited to spend time together without the screen between them. The thought of being with him, even temporarily, filled her with anticipation and hope.

And as she boarded the plane, a smile on her face and her heart brimming with love, Emma knew that whatever the future held, she was ready to face it—together with Ethan.

Chapter 15: A City of Dreams

Emma stepped off the plane, her heart racing as she made her way through the bustling airport. Her fingers curled around the strap of her bag, knuckles white, as a hundred what-ifs swirled in her mind—hope and hesitation walking side by side. She scanned the crowd eagerly, and when she finally spotted Ethan waiting near the arrivals, her breath caught. He looked tired but radiant, his face lighting up as their eyes met. She hurried towards him, her heart pounding as he pulled her into his arms.

"You're here," he murmured, his voice a mixture of disbelief and joy. "I've missed you so much."

She smiled, feeling the weight of the weeks apart melt away in his embrace. "I missed you too."

They spent the drive to his apartment catching up, laughing and holding hands as if they were teenagers in love. The city lights cast a warm glow over them, and for the first time since their separation, Emma felt truly at ease. New York buzzed with energy, and she felt as though their reunion had breathed new life into her.

Ethan had taken time off work for the weekend, and they planned to explore the city together. That first night, he cooked dinner in his apartment, a cozy, modern space with big windows that overlooked the bustling streets below. They shared a simple meal, talking about everything and nothing, relishing the luxury of not having to say goodbye after just a few hours.

The next morning, they strolled hand-in-hand through Central Park, taking in the autumn colours and the crisp air. The park was alive with people—joggers, families, tourists—and Emma couldn't help but feel a thrill at the thought of this new chapter in her life. Ethan showed her his favourite spots in the city: a small jazz bar tucked away in Greenwich Village, a quiet bookstore in Brooklyn, and a little café that made the best chai latte she'd ever tasted.

Their time together was perfect, almost dreamlike. Yet, as the days passed, Emma began to notice the subtle differences between them—like how he no longer lingered over breakfast, or how his gaze drifted to his phone during their walks through the park. Each moment, small and quiet, nudged her toward the truth that something beneath their surface had shifted. Ethan was deeply immersed in his work life, his schedule driven by meetings, client calls, and project deadlines. While he was attentive and devoted to her, she could see that his focus was split, his mind often lingering on work even in their quietest moments.

One evening, as they shared a late dinner in his apartment, Ethan's phone buzzed with a work notification. He glanced at the screen, his face tightening slightly.

"I'm sorry, Emma. Just one second," he murmured, tapping out a quick reply.

Emma forced a smile, telling herself she understood. His job was demanding, and she admired his dedication. But as he typed, she felt a pang of loneliness—a reminder that while they were together, there was still a part of his life that she couldn't fully share.

When he finished, he looked up, noticing her expression. "Hey, you alright?"

She hesitated, choosing her words carefully. "I guess... it's just hard sometimes. You're here, but sometimes it feels like you're not." Her voice trembled, and she looked down at her plate, pushing a piece of food around with her fork. It took everything in her not to retreat into silence again—she had promised herself she would speak up, even when it was hard.

He looked at her, his face softening with understanding. "Emma, I'm sorry. I know it's hard. This job, this city— it's a lot. But I want you to know that you're my priority. I just need time to find that balance."

Emma nodded, reaching across the table to take his hand. "I know, Ethan. I just... I don't want us to lose each other to the distance, even when we're together."

He held her hand, his gaze sincere. "We won't. I promise. I'm learning, too. I want to make this work just as much as you do."

[81]

They shared a quiet moment, the noise of the city humming around them, a reminder of the world outside their little bubble. Emma felt a renewed sense of commitment, a willingness to adapt, to be patient, and to face the challenges of this life together.

As the weekend came to an end, they spent their final day visiting the art galleries in SoHo. Emma marveled at the eclectic displays, the vibrant artwork that told stories of love, loss, and hope. She found herself imagining a life here—a life where she could immerse herself in the city's creative energy, just as she had once dreamed back in college, when she and Ethan used to sketch ideas for their future on napkins in tiny cafés, believing anything was possible, perhaps even find a way to pursue her own passion for writing and art.

In a quiet corner of one gallery, Ethan pulled her close, his arm around her waist as they admired a painting together. "You'd be incredible here, you know," he murmured, his voice soft. "I can see you fitting right in—meeting artists, exploring new ideas. You'd thrive."

Emma looked up at him, her heart swelling. "Maybe," she replied thoughtfully, the hint of a smile tugging at her lips. "It's hard to imagine leaving everything behind, but… I can see the appeal."

He took her hands, his gaze earnest. "Emma, I don't want you to feel pressured to make a decision. I'll wait as long as you need. But I want you to know that, whatever you choose, I'm here."

[82]

As they walked back to his apartment, Emma's mind raced with possibilities. She could feel her heart pulling in two directions: one toward the familiar life she had in her hometown, and the other toward the unknown, filled with promise and the possibility of a life with Ethan. She knew the decision wouldn't come easily, but for the first time, she felt a spark of excitement about the future they might create together.

That night, as they lay tangled in each other's arms, Ethan whispered softly, "I don't want you to leave tomorrow."

Emma's heart ached, a bittersweet feeling settling within her. "I don't want to leave either."

They fell asleep holding each other, the city outside buzzing with life as they shared their last moments before her flight. When morning came, she felt the heaviness of parting, but also a quiet resolve. This wasn't the end—it was simply another chapter in their journey.

At the airport, Ethan kissed her deeply, his arms wrapped around her as if to keep her close, even across the miles.

"Come back soon," he murmured, his voice rough with emotion.

"I will," she replied, her eyes meeting his. "And I'll think about… everything. About us, and what the future could be."

As she boarded the plane, Emma glanced back, seeing him watching her from a distance. She felt a swell of love, knowing that no matter where they were, their connection was strong enough to withstand the miles between them.

As the plane lifted off, she closed her eyes, her mind racing with thoughts of New York, of the life she might have here with Ethan, of the dreams she hadn't yet explored. She felt a quiet certainty settle within her—the belief that, whatever her decision, it would be made out of love, not fear. It was like watching the horizon emerge from morning mist—still distant, but clear enough to move toward with steady steps.

And as the city disappeared below her, Emma knew that she was ready to face whatever came next, trusting that her heart would guide her toward the path she was meant to take.

Chapter 16: The Crossroads

Back home, Emma felt both grateful and restless. The visit to New York had been a whirlwind of emotions, and she couldn't shake the lingering memory of Ethan's embrace, his whispered words as he held her at the airport. Now, her familiar life seemed different—tinged with a subtle restlessness, as though it no longer quite fit. She found herself pausing mid-task, distracted during meetings, her thoughts drifting to possibilities that had once felt too far away to name.

Her friends noticed the change immediately. Over lunch, Lucy eyed her curiously, finally breaking the silence with a gentle nudge. "So, New York looked good on you. I can tell there's something on your mind."

Emma smiled, stirring her tea as she considered her answer. "It's just… everything feels different. New York has this energy, this sense of possibility. Being with Ethan, I felt like we could build something real. But then there's this part of me that wonders if I'm ready to let go of everything here."

Lucy nodded thoughtfully. "Sometimes, the hardest decisions are between two good things. You have your life here, your friends, your career. But love? That's something rare."

Emma looked down, a swell of emotion tightening her chest. "I do love him, Lucy. But I also love my life here. I just don't know if I can have both."

Lucy reached across the table, her voice gentle. "Maybe it's not about choosing between the two. Maybe it's about finding a way to make them work together."

Over the next few days, Emma threw herself into her routines, seeking clarity in the familiar. She went to work, spent evenings with friends, and returned to her volunteer hours at the animal shelter. Yet, each moment felt layered with an undercurrent of tension, as if she were waiting for something to reveal the right answer to her dilemma.

One afternoon, as she sat in her favourite park, she pulled out her notebook, the pages filled with thoughts and reflections from her recent trip. She flipped to a blank page and began writing, letting her feelings pour out in a stream of consciousness.

What would it mean to stay? she wrote. It meant comfort, security, a life she knew and loved. Here, she had friends, routines, and a deep sense of belonging.

And what would it mean to go? She imagined life in New York—new experiences, challenges, and the thrill of starting fresh with someone she loved. She could see herself growing, expanding, creating something entirely new.

She paused, feeling a weight lift slightly as she saw her feelings written out on the page. She realised that her struggle wasn't just about staying or going. It was like standing on the edge of a river, watching two currents pull in different directions—familiarity to one side, and growth to the other—and knowing she could no longer straddle both banks. It was about embracing change, about trusting that love could guide her through the uncertainty.

Just then, her phone buzzed with a message from Ethan.

Ethan: Hey, just wanted to let you know I've been thinking about you. I know this isn't easy, but whatever you decide, I'm here.

Emma felt a surge of warmth, reminded once again of the patience and love Ethan had shown her throughout this journey. His words were gentle, reassuring, free of pressure or expectation, and she knew he meant every one of them.

That evening, she called him, needing to hear his voice. When he picked up, his familiar warmth instantly filled the distance between them.

"Hey," he said softly. "I wasn't expecting a call, but I'm glad to hear from you."

"I just… I wanted to talk," she replied, her voice tentative. "I've been thinking about us. About the future."

He was silent for a moment, waiting for her to continue.

"Ethan, I love you," she began, her voice trembling slightly. Her chest tightened as the words left her lips, echoing a moment from their early days when she had almost said it but held back. Now, saying it aloud felt like crossing a threshold she had waited years to reach. "And I don't want to lose what we have. But I'm also afraid—afraid of leaving behind everything I've built here, of not being able to make a life in New York."

Ethan's voice was gentle as he replied, "Emma, I don't expect you to give up your life. I know this is a huge decision, and I'm here for you, no matter what. We can figure this out together."

She took a deep breath, feeling the tension within her begin to ease. "Thank you. I think… I just need a bit more time to make peace with whatever choice I make. But I want you to know that I'm leaning toward being with you. I just want to make sure it's for the right reasons, that I'm not just running away from my own fears."

Ethan's voice softened. "Emma, whatever you decide, I trust you. Take all the time you need. And when you're ready, I'll be here."

Over the next few days, Emma immersed herself in reflection, seeking clarity in her heart. She sought counsel from friends, spent hours journaling, and even took long walks alone, allowing herself to fully explore her feelings.

Finally, after a week of soul-searching, she reached a quiet decision. It came to her during a morning walk through the park, when she saw a young couple laughing on a bench, their joy unguarded and free. In that moment, she realised that the life she wanted was one where love wasn't postponed or rationed—it was lived fully, every day, one that felt both thrilling and terrifying. She realised that, while her life here was comfortable, there was something inside her that longed for more—a life of growth, change, and adventure. And she knew that Ethan was part of that journey.

That evening, she called Ethan, her heart steady and her voice calm. "Ethan, I've made a decision."

His voice was filled with anticipation. "I'm listening."

"I want to be with you," she said softly. "I want to take this leap of faith. I don't have all the answers, and I know there will be challenges, but I don't want to live with regrets. I love you, and I'm ready to build a life together."

Ethan's voice broke slightly, filled with emotion. "Emma… you have no idea how much this means to me. I promise you, we'll make this work. We'll find our way, one step at a time."

As they shared their hopes and plans, Emma felt a newfound sense of excitement and peace, as if she were finally stepping into the life she was meant to live. She knew there would be challenges, moments of doubt, and difficult days. But with Ethan by her side, she felt ready to face it all.

That night, she began making plans, taking the first steps toward a new life. And as she looked forward to the future, she knew that, while the road ahead might be uncertain, she stood at its beginning like a sunrise-warmed path stretching into the unknown—wide open, inviting, and wholly hers to walk her heart was certain of one thing: she was exactly where she was meant to be.

Chapter 17: Farewells and Fresh Starts

The days following Emma's decision felt like a whirlwind. Once the choice had been made, everything seemed to move quickly, as if the universe itself were ushering her toward her new life. She began organising her apartment, packing up memories and deciding what to bring with her and what to leave behind. Each item, each decision felt like a small farewell to the life she was letting go—like turning the pages of a well-loved book, knowing the chapter had ended but the story would stay with her forever.

Lucy, ever the supportive friend, showed up one Saturday morning with coffee and a stack of empty boxes. "Alright, girl," she said, setting the coffee on the table with a grin. "Let's get packing."

Emma smiled, feeling a mixture of gratitude and melancholy as they worked side by side, sorting through years' worth of memories. Together, they carefully wrapped framed photos, folded clothes into neat piles, and reminisced over the little mementos she'd collected through the years.

"Remember this?" Lucy asked, holding up an old photo of them dressed as 80s rock stars for a costume party.

Emma laughed, the sound a little wistful. "That was one of the best nights of my life. I'll never forget it."

As they continued packing, Emma felt the weight of each memory, each cherished moment with friends, family, and her familiar routines. But mixed with the sadness was a quiet thrill—a sense of anticipation for the new life awaiting her. She knew that while she was leaving behind a lot, she was also carrying the most important parts with her.

That evening, her friends threw her a farewell party, a small gathering at her favourite café. As she entered the room, she was greeted with cheers, laughter, and hugs from the people who had been her support system through all the highs and lows of recent years.

Lucy raised a glass, her voice warm and affectionate. "Here's to Emma, the bravest woman I know. You're starting a new chapter, but we're with you every step of the way. And Ethan better know how lucky he is!"

Everyone laughed, clinking their glasses and sharing stories of their favourite memories with Emma. The evening was filled with laughter, a few tears, and promises to visit. By the end of the night, she felt surrounded by love, her heart full from the kindness and encouragement of her friends.

After the party, as she walked back to her nearly empty apartment, Emma felt a bittersweet ache settle within her. She knew she was making the right choice, but the weight of leaving behind her friends and her familiar world was more profound than she'd expected. She spent that night alone, sitting on her living room floor surrounded by boxes, reflecting on everything she was about to leave behind.

The following week, Ethan arrived to help her with the final stages of her move. Seeing him in her hometown felt surreal, as though her two worlds were blending together for a brief, fleeting moment. They spent the day packing up the last few items, making arrangements for the moving truck, and planning the logistics of her transition.

As they worked, Emma felt a sense of peace settle within her. Being with Ethan in this space, in the life she'd known for so long, made her feel grounded, as if she were truly bringing the best parts of her past into her future.

That evening, they took one last walk through the neighbourhood, stopping by her favourite park. The sun was setting, casting a warm, golden glow over the familiar paths and trees. Emma took a deep breath, letting the beauty of her hometown fill her one last time.

"You ready for this?" Ethan asked, his hand warm around hers.

She looked up at him, a soft smile on her face. "I think so. It's hard to leave, but I know it's time."

They walked in silence for a few moments, the weight of the moment settling between them. Finally, Ethan stopped, pulling her into a gentle embrace. "Emma, thank you for choosing this—for choosing us. I know it wasn't easy."

She wrapped her arms around him, resting her head on his shoulder. "You're worth it, Ethan. This new life we're building together… it's worth it."

As they stood there, holding each other in the quiet evening light, Emma felt the last remnants of doubt fade away. She was ready—not just for the move, but for the adventure, the unknown, the promise of love that lay ahead.

The next morning, as they loaded up the last of her belongings and prepared to leave, Emma took one final look at her apartment, her heart filled with gratitude. She knew she was stepping into something new, something that would challenge her and help her grow in ways she couldn't yet imagine. Just months ago, she had been paralyzed by uncertainty, afraid to make any move that might disrupt her fragile sense of stability. Now, she was choosing change—choosing love—not because it was easy, but because she was finally brave enough to believe she could thrive in it. But she also knew that, wherever life took her, the love she carried would be her anchor, her guide, her constant.

As they drove away, with the city slowly disappearing in the rearview mirror, Emma held Ethan's hand, feeling the thrill of a new beginning. Her past, her memories, her friendships—all of it was woven into the fabric of who she was, guiding her toward a future she was finally ready to embrace.

And as they merged onto the highway, bound for New York, she felt a quiet certainty settle within her, a sense that she was exactly where she was meant to be—moving forward, with love and hope lighting the way.

The energy of New York was palpable the moment Emma arrived. The noise, the movement, the endless rhythm of the city—it was everything Ethan had described and more. As they drove through the bustling streets toward his apartment, she watched the towering buildings, the sea of people, and the vibrant billboards illuminating the city. Her heart raced with a mixture of excitement and nervousness.

When they reached his apartment, Ethan helped her carry the last of her belongings inside, and they both collapsed onto the couch, breathless from the effort and laughter.

"Welcome to your new home," he said, his smile warm and full of pride.

Emma looked around, her gaze lingering on the spacious apartment. Her eyes landed on the windows where the city lights blinked like distant stars, and for a brief moment, she remembered the tiny kitchen back home where she'd once imagined this very life. A lump rose in her throat—half grief, half joy—as she took it all in with its big windows overlooking the busy street below. "It's perfect, Ethan. I still can't believe I'm actually here."

He leaned in, brushing a soft kiss against her forehead. "You're here, Emma. We're here. Together."

The next few days were a whirlwind of unpacking, organising, and settling into their shared space. They spent each day rearranging furniture, hanging up photos, and blending their two worlds into one. Emma brought her favourite books, plants, and trinkets from her hometown, each item making the apartment feel a little more like home.

Ethan had taken time off work to help her settle in, and they spent their evenings exploring the city. They strolled through Central Park, enjoyed late-night pizza from a small corner pizzeria, and even took an evening boat ride along the Hudson River, watching the city lights glimmer against the dark water. Each new experience was exhilarating, and Emma felt herself falling in love with the city as she fell even deeper in love with Ethan.

One afternoon, as they sat together at a café near their apartment, Emma looked out at the bustling street, a smile tugging at her lips. "I think I'm going to like it here," she said, her voice filled with wonder.

Ethan grinned, reaching across the table to hold her hand. "New York looks good on you."

Yet, as the days went by and Ethan returned to work, Emma began to experience the subtle reality of her new life. The bustling street below buzzed with urgency, a stark contrast to the stillness of the apartment that now felt cavernous in Ethan's absence. While she enjoyed the thrill of exploration, the bustling pace of the city often left her feeling overwhelmed. New York had a way of swallowing people up, its vastness and intensity sometimes making her feel like a small fish in a vast, churning ocean.

With Ethan back to his demanding schedule, Emma found herself alone in the apartment for long stretches of time. She busied herself with errands, unpacking, and setting up her new home office, but there were moments when the silence pressed down on her, a stark contrast to the lively city outside. She missed her friends, her old neighbourhood, and the familiarity of her hometown.

Determined to find her place in this new world, Emma began venturing out on her own. She signed up for a writing workshop at a local bookstore, hoping to meet people with similar interests. She explored the city's museums, parks, and coffee shops, finding small pockets of peace amid the city's relentless pace.

One evening, as she was returning from a day of exploring, she received a text from Lucy.

Lucy: How's my city girl doing? Missing you like crazy here.

Emma smiled, her heart swelling with warmth at the sight of her friend's message.

[97]

Emma: It's incredible here, but a bit overwhelming. Can't lie—I miss you too. Need to plan a visit soon!

Lucy: You name the date, and I'm there. Also… tell me everything!

That night, Emma called Lucy, sharing stories of her adventures and her quiet struggles with adjusting to the city. Lucy listened, offering encouragement and reminding her that it was okay to feel a little lost at first. By the time they ended the call, Emma felt reassured, comforted by the knowledge that her friends back home were still with her, even across the miles.

As the days turned into weeks, Emma found herself slowly adapting to her new life. She discovered her favourite coffee shop just a few blocks from their apartment, a quiet spot where she could write and people-watch. She met people in her writing workshop who shared her passion for stories, forming new friendships that brought a sense of belonging.

One evening, after a particularly long day at work, Ethan came home to find Emma sitting on the balcony, a cup of tea in her hands as she watched the city lights.

"Hey," he said, stepping outside to join her. "How was your day?"

Emma smiled, shifting to make space for him. "It was good. I feel like I'm finally settling in. I made a friend in my writing class—her name's Anna, and she invited me to join a book club. I think I'm starting to find my place here."

Ethan wrapped an arm around her, pulling her close as they looked out over the city together. "I knew you'd make it, Emma. New York is lucky to have you."

She leaned her head against his shoulder, a wave of contentment washing over her. "I'm lucky to have you. None of this would be possible without you."

They sat in comfortable silence, the hum of the city below a soothing backdrop to their thoughts. Emma felt a profound sense of gratitude for the journey they had taken to reach this point—the doubts, the struggles, and the love that had guided them through it all.

As the weeks turned into months, Emma continued to build her life in New York, filling it with new friends, new experiences, and new dreams. She discovered a vibrant writing community, joined an art class that reignited her creativity, and began working on a personal project she'd long dreamed of—a book of short stories inspired by her journey of self-discovery and love.

And through it all, Ethan was by her side, his presence a steady anchor in the whirlwind of her new life. They faced the challenges of city life together—the long work hours, the packed schedules, and the occasional loneliness that came with living in a place so vast. Yet, each challenge only seemed to bring them closer, strengthening the bond they had fought so hard to rebuild.

One evening, as they sat together on the balcony, watching the sun set over the skyline, Ethan took her hand, his gaze filled with warmth and pride.

"Emma," he began softly, "I just want you to know how proud I am of you. You took a huge leap, and I know it wasn't easy. But you're making a life here. You're creating something beautiful."

Emma's heart swelled, tears glistening in her eyes. "Thank you, Ethan. I couldn't have done any of this without you. You're the reason I had the courage to try."

They sat together, wrapped in each other's warmth, as the city lights flickered on around them. In that moment, Emma felt a profound sense of peace, knowing that she was exactly where she was meant to be. The journey had been long, and the road ahead would hold its own challenges, but she was ready—ready to face whatever came next, with Ethan by her side and New York as their backdrop.

As the stars began to fill the sky, Emma felt a quiet thrill of anticipation, a sense that her life was just beginning, filled with endless possibilities. And with a heart full of love and a spirit ready for adventure, she stepped onto the balcony once more, the city lights winking back at her like promises yet to be written. The future stretched before her—vast, unwritten, and sparkling like the skyline she was slowly learning to call home.

Chapter 18: Dreams and Decisions

As winter set in, New York transformed into a city of twinkling lights and bustling holiday markets. Emma found herself enchanted by the magic of the season, bundled up in scarves and gloves as she explored the city's festive displays and icy parks. Her life had taken on a comfortable rhythm, with morning walks to the corner café, afternoons spent writing by the window, and evenings curled up beside Ethan with a book in hand. Each day felt like a step further into her new beginning.

Her writing workshop had led to connections she hadn't anticipated. Through her new friend Anna, she'd been introduced to a few editors and authors in the city, which had opened doors Emma hadn't even thought possible. She'd begun attending literary events and book signings, immersing herself in the world of storytelling that had once been only a distant dream.

One afternoon, while browsing a local bookstore with Anna, Emma's phone buzzed. The number was unfamiliar, but she picked up, her curiosity piqued.

"Hello, is this Emma?" a woman's warm voice asked.

"Yes, this is she."

"Emma, this is Sarah Hargrove. I'm an editor at The New Yorker. We received a short story submission from you through Anna, and I wanted to personally reach out to let you know it made quite an impression on us."

Emma's breath caught, her heart racing. "Oh! Wow— thank you. I'm… thrilled to hear that."

"Well, we'd like to discuss the possibility of publishing it," Sarah continued, her tone encouraging. "And, if you're interested, I'd love to speak to you about contributing regularly. Your voice has a unique quality—there's a depth and honesty to it that we think our readers would connect with."

Emma could hardly contain her excitement. "I'd be absolutely honoured, Sarah. I've always admired The New Yorker. This is… it's a dream come true."

They arranged a meeting for later that week, and Emma hung up, still reeling. She turned to Anna, her eyes wide with disbelief. "That was The New Yorker. They want to publish my story!"

Anna hugged her, beaming with pride. "Emma, that's incredible! You deserve this. Your work is amazing."

Emma floated through the next few days, unable to keep the smile from her face. She hummed while preparing her morning coffee, paused to greet neighbours with unexpected warmth, and found herself dancing around the apartment when no one was watching—her joy spilling into even the quietest corners of her day. She shared the news with Ethan, who pulled her into a tight embrace, his pride evident.

"I'm so happy for you, Emma. You're making your mark here, and it's only the beginning," he said, his voice full of admiration.

At her meeting with Sarah, the editor was warm and encouraging. They discussed her story in detail, and as the conversation flowed, Sarah hinted at the potential for Emma to contribute regularly to the magazine. The idea both thrilled and intimidated her. A regular position at a prestigious publication like The New Yorker was a rare opportunity, one that could elevate her writing career to new heights.

But as she walked back home, the weight of the decision settled on her, like a coat too heavy for the early winter air—comforting in its significance, but burdensome in its unknowns. She knew the job would demand her full attention, possibly requiring long hours, tight deadlines, and the energy to constantly create fresh content. Balancing that with her new life in New York—and her relationship with Ethan—felt daunting.

That evening, as they cooked dinner together, Emma shared her concerns with Ethan. "This opportunity is huge, but I'm worried about how it might affect us. A regular position would mean longer hours, and I don't want my career to come between us."

Ethan set down the knife he'd been using to chop vegetables, turning to face her. "Emma, I don't want you to hold back because of me. This is your dream—don't let anything stop you from pursuing it. We'll find a way to make it work, no matter what."

She sighed, resting her head against his shoulder. "Thank you. I just want to make sure I don't lose sight of what's important."

Ethan wrapped an arm around her, pulling her close. "Emma, we've come this far together. I'm not going anywhere, and I know you're not either. We'll figure it out."

Encouraged by his words, Emma took the job. The weeks that followed were a whirlwind of writing, deadlines, and late nights. She found herself fully immersed in her work, each assignment both challenging and fulfilling. Her first story was published, and seeing her name in The New Yorker was a moment she would never forget—a reminder of how far she'd come and the dreams she'd finally dared to pursue.

Yet, the demands of her job did create strain. There were times when she was too tired to go out, or when she had to cancel plans with Ethan to meet a deadline. While he was always supportive and understanding, she could sense the subtle changes in their relationship, the moments of frustration that lingered between them.

One evening, after a particularly long day, Ethan brought up the topic as they shared a quiet dinner.

"Emma, I'm so proud of you. But I miss us—the little things we used to do together," he admitted, his voice gentle but honest. "I feel like your job is taking more of you than I am."

His words hit her heart, and she felt a pang of guilt. She reached across the table, taking his hand in hers. "I know, and I'm sorry. I don't want you to feel that way. I'm still figuring out how to balance everything, but I promise I'll work on it."

They spent the rest of the evening talking openly about their hopes and concerns, and somewhere between the fears and the reassurances, Emma realised something essential: their love had become a partnership built on truth, not just affection. For the first time, she saw their challenges not as threats, but as invitations to grow— together. sharing their fears and finding comfort in each other's words. It was a reminder of the importance of communication, of being honest even when it was hard.

As the months passed, Emma gradually learned to balance her career and her relationship. She carved out time for herself and for Ethan, setting boundaries with work and prioritising the moments they shared. They began dedicating one evening a week to "just them"—a night free from work and distractions, where they could reconnect and nurture the love that had brought them to this point.

[106]

The changes paid off, and Emma felt a renewed sense of harmony in her life. She continued to write for The New Yorker, her stories gaining recognition, and each time Ethan read her latest work, his pride and admiration only grew.

One evening, as they walked through the city hand in hand, Ethan paused, looking at her with a soft smile.

"Emma, I want you to know how proud I am of you. You're building an incredible life here, one that you've earned. And every time I see your name in print, I'm reminded of how lucky I am to be a part of your story."

Emma felt her heart swell, a warmth spreading through her chest. "I'm the lucky one, Ethan. You've been my constant through all of this. Thank you for believing in me, even when I struggled to believe in myself."

They continued their walk, the city lights casting a soft glow around them. Emma felt a sense of contentment, a quiet joy that came from knowing she was living the life she'd always dreamed of—one filled with love, purpose, and the courage to chase her dreams.

And as they walked through the bustling streets of New York, weaving through the crowd like two threads in a tapestry yet unfinished,, surrounded by the pulse of the city, she knew that her journey was just beginning. With Ethan by her side and her passion guiding her, she felt ready to face whatever lay ahead, confident that together, they could conquer anything.

Chapter 19: A Future Together

As spring blossomed in New York, Emma found herself settling into a comfortable rhythm. Her work with The New Yorker had become a rewarding, albeit demanding, part of her life, and she felt a renewed sense of confidence and fulfillment. Her relationship with Ethan was thriving as well, the two of them finding harmony despite the challenges of balancing work, love, and city life.

One evening, as they shared dinner in a small, candle-lit bistro tucked away in Greenwich Village, Ethan looked at her with a smile that hinted at something deeper.

"I've been thinking," he began, his voice soft but steady, "about the future. About us."

Emma's heart skipped a beat, sensing the weight of his words. "What about us?"

He reached across the table, taking her hand in his. "Emma, I know our lives have changed so much since you moved here. And I love every moment with you. But I want to take that next step with you—something permanent."

Her heart raced, a warm thrill spreading through her as she absorbed his words. In that moment, flashes of their journey together—quiet coffees, tearful nights, the long walk through Central Park that changed everything—

rushed through her mind, anchoring his promise in a hundred small memories that made it feel even more real. She'd imagined a future with Ethan before, but hearing him say it out loud made it real, tangible. "Are you… are you talking about marriage?"

Ethan smiled, his eyes filled with a gentle certainty. "Yes. I want us to build a life together, a home, a family someday, if that's what you want. I want you to know that, whatever the future holds, I'm committed to it. To us."

Emma felt a swell of emotion, a mixture of joy and excitement. She took a deep breath, her heart pounding as she looked into his eyes. "Ethan, I want that too. I never thought I'd be here, but with you, I feel ready. I can imagine our future together."

They shared a quiet moment, the noise of the restaurant fading as they focused on each other, Ethan's thumb gently tracing the back of her hand, their breath syncing in a rhythm only they could feel—an unspoken promise humming between them, lost in the shared vision of their future. That night, as they walked home hand in hand, they spoke of their dreams, their hopes for a life together, and the adventures they wanted to share.

In the weeks that followed, Ethan began making plans to propose. Emma knew a proposal was coming, but he kept the details a mystery, determined to surprise her. Their excitement grew, filling their days with a joyful anticipation.

One weekend, he invited her to the Catskills for a short getaway, a retreat from the bustling pace of the city. The cabin he'd rented was nestled among pine trees, overlooking a serene lake. They spent their days hiking and their nights stargazing, soaking in the peace and solitude of nature.

On their last evening there, as the sun began to set, Ethan suggested they take one last walk by the lake. The sky was painted in hues of pink and gold, the reflection shimmering on the water's surface like a mirror to her own calm—serene, expectant, and touched by something sacred she couldn't quite name. As they walked along the shore, Ethan suddenly paused, turning to face her.

"Emma," he began, his voice filled with emotion, "being with you has changed my life in ways I can't even describe. You are my best friend, my inspiration, my love. And I don't want to spend another day without you by my side."

With a gentle smile, he reached into his pocket, pulling out a small, velvet box. Opening it, he revealed a simple yet elegant ring that sparkled in the fading light. "Will you marry me?"

Emma's eyes filled with tears, her heart swelling as she looked at him, the man who had been her constant, her anchor through every change, every challenge. "Yes," she whispered, her voice thick with emotion. "Yes, Ethan, a thousand times yes."

He slipped the ring onto her finger, and they shared a kiss filled with love and the promise of a future together. They stood there, wrapped in each other's arms, as the sun dipped below the horizon, the lake bathed in a soft twilight glow.

Returning to New York, they were greeted with cheers and congratulations from their friends and family, each person sharing in their joy and excitement. Over the following weeks, they began making plans, deciding on a simple wedding surrounded by the people who mattered most to them.

Their days were filled with a flurry of activity—selecting a venue, choosing invitations, and planning a small but meaningful celebration. Emma found herself filled with a joyful energy, the anticipation of their future lighting up every moment. Even tasks she once found daunting— like finalising guest lists or navigating tricky family dynamics—now felt like steps in a dance she was eager to learn.

One evening, as they sat on the balcony of their apartment, watching the city lights twinkle below, Emma turned to Ethan with a smile. "Can you believe we're here? That we're really doing this?"

Ethan took her hand, his eyes warm and full of love. "I can believe it. I knew from the moment you moved here that we would end up here. We've built this life together, and now we get to build a home."

Their wedding day arrived on a sunny afternoon in early summer. They exchanged vows in a small garden surrounded by their closest friends and family. Emma wore a simple dress, her hair adorned with fresh flowers, and Ethan looked at her with a love so profound it took her breath away.

As they exchanged rings, Emma felt a sense of peace and joy unlike anything she'd ever known. She knew that their journey hadn't been easy, that they'd faced countless challenges to reach this point. But she also knew that every step had been worth it, that they were exactly where they were meant to be—together.

After the ceremony, they celebrated with their loved ones under twinkling fairy lights, sharing laughter, stories, and dreams for the future. And as the night came to a close, they stood together, looking out at the city that had become their home, their hearts full of love and gratitude for the journey that had brought them here.

As they began their life as husband and wife, Emma felt a quiet thrill of anticipation for the future. She knew there would be new challenges, new adventures, and new dreams. But with Ethan by her side, she felt ready to face it all, knowing that together, they could conquer anything.

And as they held each other under the stars, Emma whispered softly, "This is just the beginning." Above them, the constellations shimmered like a map of unwritten stories, the night sky stretching wide with promise, echoing the limitless journey ahead.

Ethan smiled, his arms wrapped around her as he replied, "Yes. And I can't wait to see where it takes us."

Chapter 20: A Life Together

Emma and Ethan returned from their honeymoon filled with a renewed sense of love and excitement. They had spent two blissful weeks exploring the rolling vineyards of Tuscany, wandering through ancient towns, and sharing intimate moments that felt like stolen pieces of forever. Now, as they stepped back into their New York apartment, it felt different—no longer just a space but a home they'd created together. The scent of lavender from their honeymoon still lingered faintly on the throw pillows, and their framed photos—sun-drenched smiles in Tuscany, laughter beneath olive trees—now graced the walls, grounding their love in something beautifully lived-in.

Their first few weeks of marriage were a joyful blend of new routines and familiar comforts. Emma loved the small, ordinary moments: waking up to Ethan's warm smile, cooking breakfast together in the early light, and returning home each evening to find him waiting with a warm embrace. Each moment felt like a precious gift, a reminder of the love that had brought them here.

One Saturday morning, as they sipped coffee together on the balcony, Ethan looked at her thoughtfully. "I've been thinking," he said, a hint of excitement in his voice, "about our future. About the life we want to build."

Emma smiled, setting her mug down as she leaned into him. "What kind of future are you imagining?"

He took her hand, his gaze warm and earnest. "I want us to have a home that feels like us—a place where we can make memories, have friends over, and maybe, someday, raise a family."

The thought filled Emma with a quiet joy, the vision of their shared dreams coming into focus. "I'd love that too, Ethan. Maybe somewhere with a bit more space, a place where we can breathe."

They began browsing listings, exploring neighborhoods that felt a little more removed from the bustling city center, with quiet streets and small parks. It became their weekend ritual, and each Sunday, they'd return home with a new vision for their future.

But as the honeymoon phase wore on, Emma and Ethan faced the everyday realities of married life. Emma often found herself pausing during the day, realising how different things felt from those golden days in Tuscany—still good, still full of love, but more complex. Ethan noticed too, quietly recognising how their perfect moments now included imperfection, and how that made them feel even more real. They discovered quirks and habits they hadn't noticed before, and while most were endearing, others required patience and compromise. Ethan tended to leave his socks around the apartment, and Emma's late-night work sessions sometimes meant he had to sleep with the light on.

One evening, after a particularly hectic day at work, Ethan came home to find Emma hunched over her laptop, her brow furrowed in concentration. She looked up as he walked in, giving him a tired smile.

"Hey," she said, reaching out for his hand. "I'm sorry—I just need to finish this article before tomorrow."

He nodded, bending down to kiss her forehead. "Take your time. I'll get started on dinner."

As he moved around the kitchen, preparing their meal, Ethan felt a wave of pride for Emma and the career she'd built. Yet, he also felt the pang of wanting more time together, a quiet longing for the simplicity they'd had before life became so busy—like those lazy mornings in Tuscany, sipping espresso in silence, their only agenda being to enjoy each other's company beneath the sun-washed sky.

After dinner, they sat on the couch, Emma resting her head on his shoulder as they talked about their day. They shared their frustrations and dreams, finding comfort in each other's presence, knowing that their relationship would continue to grow and evolve as they faced each challenge together.

Over the coming months, they found their balance, learning how to prioritize their relationship amid their busy schedules. They set aside time each week for date nights, mini adventures, and quiet evenings at home. Their weekends were filled with laughter, exploring art galleries, hiking trails, and quiet dinners where they dreamed about their future.

One Sunday morning, as they browsed through a small neighborhood just outside the city, they stumbled upon a charming townhouse. The house had tall windows, a cozy garden, and a warmth that felt like home. They exchanged a glance, a spark of excitement in their eyes as they stepped inside. Emma felt a flutter in her chest—not just excitement, but a quiet sense of rightness, as though they were crossing a threshold into a chapter they had both unknowingly been writing toward for years.

The rooms were filled with natural light, and the layout was open yet cozy, with plenty of space for gatherings and quiet evenings alike. By the time they left, they knew they'd found something special.

Two months later, they moved into their new home, filling it with their favorite books, artwork, and mementos from their travels. It became a space where they could grow together, a sanctuary from the noise and demands of city life.

One evening, as they sat in their garden, watching the stars emerge in the night sky, Ethan turned to Emma, a soft smile on his face. "I feel like this is the start of something incredible, Emma. I never imagined I'd be this happy, that I'd get to share my life with someone as wonderful as you."

Emma reached for his hand, her heart swelling with love and gratitude. "You've made my life so full, Ethan. I don't know what the future holds, but I know that, with you, it will be beautiful."

Their life together settled into a rhythm, one filled with moments both big and small, laughter and quiet contentment. They continued to nurture their dreams— Emma writing stories that touched readers, and Ethan expanding his career while finding joy in their shared life.

The years ahead would bring new challenges, new dreams, and new adventures, but they faced each day with the strength of their love and the quiet certainty that, together, they could conquer anything.

And as they sat there, under the blanket of stars in their new home, Emma felt a deep, abiding peace. She knew that their love was a journey, one filled with change, growth, and boundless joy—like a path winding through wildflower fields and forests, sometimes steep and shadowed, but always leading them back to one another. They had found their way to each other, and in each other, they had found home.

Chapter 21: Building Dreams

Emma and Ethan had been living in their new home for nearly a year, each room filled with mementos of their journey, laughter, and love. Life had settled into a steady rhythm, one that was both comforting and exciting as they continued to grow together—mornings spent sipping coffee while reading the paper, evenings filled with shared playlists and cooking experiments, and weekends exploring new corners of the city, always hand in hand. But as spring approached, life offered them both an unexpected opportunity.

One afternoon, while Emma was wrapping up her work, her editor, Sarah, called with news. "Emma, we're expanding our team, and I'd like you to consider taking on a senior role. It's an opportunity to not only write but to mentor new writers, shaping the future of the magazine."

Emma felt a thrill at the prospect, but the idea of increased responsibility came with the weight of longer hours and a more demanding schedule. She knew it was an incredible opportunity, but it also meant that her life would get even busier. She thought back to the early days of their relationship, when long hours had left her drained and disconnected, struggling to find balance between ambition and togetherness. This time, she was determined not to repeat that pattern.

That evening, she shared the news with Ethan as they prepared dinner. His face lit up with pride as he listened, but she could sense the questions lingering in his gaze.

"This is huge, Emma," he said, slicing vegetables as she stirred a pot on the stove. "You've worked so hard for this. But... are you sure it's what you want?"

Emma paused, thinking over his words. "I'm not sure yet. I love the idea of mentoring others, but I don't want it to come at the expense of our life together. We've built something beautiful here, and I don't want my career to overshadow that."

He reached for her hand, giving it a reassuring squeeze. "Whatever you decide, I'm with you. But maybe this is a chance for us to think about our future. What do we want our life to look like? Our family?"

His words stayed with her, stirring thoughts she'd been contemplating more often lately—the idea of starting a family, of growing their life together beyond their careers and shared dreams.

The following weekend, they decided to escape the city for a few days, renting a cabin in the mountains. Surrounded by nature, they took long walks, talked for hours, and dreamed together, exploring the possibilities of what their future could be.

One crisp morning, as they hiked up a winding trail, Ethan paused, looking out over the valley below, his gaze thoughtful. "Emma, I've been thinking… about us, about our future. Do you think we're ready to start a family?"

The question hung in the cool morning air, and Emma felt her heart quicken. She turned to him, seeing the hope in his eyes. "I think… I think I am. It's something I've been wanting too, but I was afraid it would mean putting my career on hold."

Ethan wrapped his arm around her, pulling her close. "You don't have to give up anything. We'll make it work, one step at a time. I want to build a life with you, Emma, one that includes everything we've dreamed of— our careers, our love, and a family."

The conversation filled her with a sense of clarity and excitement, like the still mountain air around them— crisp, wide open, and echoing with possibility. They spent the rest of the weekend dreaming together, discussing how they could balance their careers with the idea of a family, knowing that it wouldn't be easy but trusting that they could face it all together.

Returning to New York, Emma felt a newfound purpose, a vision of the life they were building together— symbolised in the way their city apartment now held both work notes and baby books, laughter echoing between ambition and the quiet hope of what was to come. She met with her editor, discussing the details of the new role, and found a way to negotiate a balance that would allow her to continue growing her career while making room for the future she wanted with Ethan.

As the months passed, Emma settled into her new role, enjoying the mentorship aspect and finding fulfillment in helping young writers discover their voices. She and Ethan continued to embrace their life together, supporting each other through the demands of their careers while keeping their shared dreams alive.

One evening, after a quiet dinner at home, Emma took a deep breath, looking across the table at Ethan. "There's something I wanted to share with you," she said, her voice trembling with emotion.

He looked at her, a smile spreading across his face as he sensed the significance of her words. "What is it?"

She reached for his hand, her eyes shining. "Ethan... I'm pregnant."

The words filled the room, and Ethan's face lit up with pure joy. He pulled her into an embrace, holding her close as they both laughed and cried, overwhelmed by the enormity of the moment.

Over the following weeks, they prepared for the arrival of their child, filling their home with the anticipation and excitement of becoming parents. They spent evenings painting the nursery, choosing names, and dreaming about the life they would share with their little one.

As Emma's due date approached, they found themselves wrapped in a quiet contentment, a sense that everything they had built together had led them to this moment. They had faced challenges, embraced change, and created a life filled with love, trust, and endless possibility.

The day finally arrived, and as Emma held their newborn daughter in her arms, she felt a depth of love she had never known before. Ethan sat beside her, his eyes filled with wonder and pride as he gazed at their child.

"She's perfect," he whispered, reaching out to gently stroke the baby's tiny hand.

Emma looked up at him, her heart full. "We're so lucky, Ethan. I couldn't have imagined a more beautiful life."

As they sat together, their daughter cradled between them, Emma felt a quiet sense of gratitude for the journey that had brought them here. She knew that life would continue to bring new challenges, but with Ethan by her side and their love as their foundation, she felt ready for whatever lay ahead.

They named their daughter Grace, a symbol of the love and hope that had guided them through every chapter of their story—just as Ethan had once said beneath the twilight sky in Tuscany, when he'd promised to build a life grounded not just in dreams, but in grace. And as they brought her home, they knew that their journey had only just begun, a new chapter filled with endless dreams, laughter, and the joy of building a family together.

Chapter 22: A New Season

The first few weeks with Grace at home were a beautiful whirlwind. Emma and Ethan's lives had been transformed overnight by the arrival of their tiny daughter, each moment bringing new surprises and lessons. Their apartment, once a quiet retreat, was now filled with the sounds of soft cries, gentle lullabies, and the joy of new beginnings. Sunlight streamed through the windows, catching on the mobile above Grace's crib, casting tiny shifting stars across the nursery walls—a visual lullaby that echoed the tender new rhythm of their life.

Emma had prepared for the challenges of parenthood, but nothing could have truly readied her for the intensity of those early days. She and Ethan took turns through the long nights, each hour a rotation of feeding, rocking, and soothing Grace back to sleep. Exhaustion became a familiar companion, but every tired moment was softened by the sight of Grace's tiny hands grasping their fingers and her sleepy eyes gazing up at them.

One afternoon, as Emma cradled Grace in her arms, Ethan walked into the nursery, holding two mugs of tea. He looked at her, his expression a mixture of love and awe. "You're amazing, you know that?"

She smiled, though weariness tugged at her eyes. "I'm just doing my best. I had no idea it would be this exhausting, but every moment feels worth it."

Ethan took a seat beside her, watching as Grace drifted off to sleep in her mother's arms. "I never knew I could feel this much love," he said softly, his gaze resting on their daughter. "It's like my heart grew three sizes overnight."

They sat together in the quiet of the nursery, sharing a moment of peace as Grace slept. Despite the sleepless nights, endless diaper changes, and constant worry that came with caring for a newborn, Emma felt her heart overflowing. She remembered the early days of their love—late-night walks, whispered promises under city lights—and realised that this love, though transformed, had only deepened. Holding Grace now, she saw the living echo of every hope they had once dared to speak aloud. She and Ethan were in this together, partners in every sense, and their love had only deepened in this new season of life.

As the weeks turned into months, they began to find their rhythm as parents. Grace's little milestones became moments of celebration: her first smile, her first time lifting her head, and the cooing sounds she made as she began to recognize their faces. Each tiny achievement filled Emma and Ethan with a joy they had never known, a reminder of the beauty in even the smallest moments.

One evening, after putting Grace to bed, they settled onto the couch, enjoying a rare moment of quiet. Ethan reached for Emma's hand, squeezing it gently.

"How are you feeling?" he asked, his voice soft and full of care.

Emma leaned her head on his shoulder, sighing. "Tired, but happy. I feel like I'm finally getting the hang of things. But there are days when it's overwhelming."

Ethan wrapped an arm around her, pulling her close. "You're doing an incredible job, Emma. I don't know how you do it—balancing Grace, work, and everything else. I'm so proud of you."

His words filled her with warmth, reminding her that she wasn't alone in this journey. They were a team, leaning on each other through the ups and downs, and she couldn't have imagined a more supportive partner.

In the months that followed, Emma gradually returned to her work, finding a way to balance her role at The New Yorker with the demands of motherhood. She set up a small home office, working while Grace napped and adjusting her schedule to fit their new life. The quiet tap of her keyboard became a rhythm of rediscovery, and the soft morning light spilling across her desk reminded her that she could still chase her passions—only now, with deeper purpose. The support from her colleagues and her editor, Sarah, allowed her to transition back on her terms, ensuring that she could remain present for Grace's early years.

Ethan, too, made adjustments, carving out time in his busy schedule to be home for dinners, playtime, and bedtime routines. They created their own family traditions: Sunday morning walks in the park, Saturday night movie marathons, and evening storytime with Grace snuggled between them.

One sunny afternoon, as they strolled through Central Park with Grace in her stroller, Ethan looked over at Emma, a contented smile on his face. "Can you believe this is our life? Sometimes I still can't believe how far we've come."

Emma reached for his hand, her own smile soft and full of love. In that brief touch, she felt the weight of their journey—the late nights, the silent tears, the whispered dreams—and marvelled at how far they'd come. This life wasn't perfect, but it was deeply, wholly theirs.. "It's incredible. I never imagined I'd be here, but I wouldn't trade this for anything. We've built something so beautiful."

They watched as Grace slept peacefully in her stroller, her tiny fists curled up, her face serene. Emma felt a deep sense of gratitude, knowing that this life—this family—was more than she had ever dreamed possible.

As Grace grew, so did their love, evolving and deepening with each new stage of parenthood. There were sleepless nights, moments of doubt, and constant adjustments, but Emma and Ethan faced each challenge hand in hand, their bond stronger than ever.

One evening, as they tucked Grace into bed and closed the nursery door, they stood together in the quiet of their home, the weight of the day finally lifting. Emma turned to Ethan, a soft smile playing on her lips. "I don't say it enough, but thank you for being here, for being my partner in this. I couldn't do this without you."

Ethan wrapped his arms around her, pulling her close. "Emma, you don't have to thank me. You're my everything. We're in this together—now and always."

They held each other, wrapped in a love that had been tested and strengthened by every step of their journey. In that moment, Emma felt a profound sense of peace, a quiet certainty that their love would continue to guide them through every season of life.

And as they stood together, watching over their sleeping daughter, they knew that their story was still unfolding, each day a new page, each moment a memory to cherish.

Emma looked up at Ethan, her heart full. "This is just the beginning, isn't it?"

He smiled, his eyes shining with love and hope. "Yes. And I can't wait to see where it takes us.

In that quiet moment, with their family gathered close, Emma felt a happiness that words could never capture— a warmth that wrapped around her like a favourite blanket on a winter morning, quiet and steady, promising that no matter what seasons came, they would face them side by side, love that would carry them through a lifetime, one beautiful day at a time.

Chapter 23: Growing Together

The years seemed to pass in the blink of an eye. One moment, Grace was a tiny newborn in their arms, and the next, she was a lively toddler, exploring the world around her with endless curiosity and joy. Emma and Ethan watched in awe as their daughter grew, especially when she surprised them by reading her first full sentence aloud, her voice steady and proud. In that moment, their amazement deepened—this little girl, once so small and new, was already discovering her voice and making her mark on the world, her laughter filling their home and her boundless energy reminding them daily of the beauty and wonder of life.

As Grace reached three years old, Emma and Ethan began to notice how much she had become her own little person. She loved books, just like her mother, often falling asleep with a story clutched tightly in her small hands. And she adored spending time with her father, following him around the house with questions about everything she encountered.

One Saturday morning, as they sat together at the breakfast table, Grace looked up at them with wide, curious eyes. "Mama, Dada, can we go to the zoo today?"

Emma exchanged a smile with Ethan, and they nodded enthusiastically. "Of course, sweetheart," Emma replied, reaching out to ruffle Grace's hair. "Let's make it a family day at the zoo."

The zoo outing was filled with laughter and awe as Grace marveled at each animal she encountered. She pressed her nose against the glass at the penguin exhibit, clapped her hands at the sight of the playful monkeys, and held tightly to both her parents' hands as they strolled past the lions, her eyes wide with fascination.

As they walked through the park, watching Grace's delight with each new discovery, Emma felt a surge of gratitude, her eyes drawn to the sunlight filtering through the leaves above them, dancing across Grace's curls like a quiet blessing. These moments—the simple, joyful days filled with laughter and love—were what she cherished most. She and Ethan had built a life together that felt like a haven, a place where they could watch their daughter grow, experience the world anew through her eyes, and feel the profound peace of family.

Later that evening, after Grace was tucked into bed, Emma and Ethan settled onto the couch, savoring the quiet that came after a busy day. Ethan wrapped his arm around her, pulling her close.

"You know," he began, his voice soft, "I still can't believe this is our life. Watching Grace today, seeing her excitement—it reminded me of how much you and I have been through to get here."

Emma smiled, leaning her head against his shoulder. "I know what you mean. Sometimes it feels like we're still those two people finding our way back to each other, just with a little more experience—and a whole lot more love."

They shared a quiet moment, reflecting on the journey that had brought them to this point—a path once uncertain, now traced like footprints in sand, sometimes washed by tides of change but always leading back to each other. Their lives had changed in ways they could never have predicted, but through it all, their love had remained the steady force guiding them forward.

Over the coming months, their lives continued to grow richer and more fulfilling. Emma found joy in watching Grace's curiosity flourish, encouraging her daughter's love for reading, art, and exploration. Ethan, too, embraced his role as a father with enthusiasm, carving out time from his busy schedule to be present for each of Grace's milestones, from her first words to her first day at preschool.

As Grace grew older, Emma and Ethan found new ways to nurture their own relationship as well. They set aside time each month for a date night, rediscovering the joy of quiet dinners, long walks, and heartfelt conversations. Their marriage became a space of growth, support, and renewed intimacy, symbolised in the way they lingered over breakfast conversations, held hands on evening walks, and left each other notes tucked into lunch bags— small acts that kept their connection tender and alive,

[133]

allowing them to be both partners and individuals, each supporting the other's dreams and ambitions.

One evening, as they sat together on the porch, watching the sun set over their neighborhood, Emma turned to Ethan, her heart full. "I can't imagine a life without this—without us."

Ethan took her hand, his gaze warm and unwavering. "Emma, you're my everything. I look at Grace, and I see our love reflected in her. I look at you, and I see my best friend, my partner, the woman who has made my life so full."

They sat together in silence, savoring the peace of the moment, their hands intertwined as they watched the sky fade from blue to a warm, gentle twilight. It was a small moment, but one filled with the quiet assurance that they were exactly where they were meant to be.

As the years continued, their family grew together, each chapter bringing new challenges and joys. Grace's world expanded, and with it, Emma and Ethan found their own lives enriched, each new experience shaping them into the parents, partners, and individuals they had always hoped to be.

Emma continued her work with The New Yorker, a dream she had nurtured since her early twenties when she'd scribble ideas in cafés, wondering if anyone would ever read her words, eventually publishing a collection of short stories inspired by her journey of love, resilience, and growth. The book resonated with readers, and Ethan couldn't have been prouder, often stopping by bookshops just to see her work on the shelves—a testament to her talent and dedication.

Ethan, too, found new opportunities in his career, but he never lost sight of what mattered most. He made sure to be home for family dinners, to read bedtime stories to Grace, and to spend quiet evenings with Emma, sharing in the life they had created together.

As they celebrated Grace's seventh birthday, surrounded by friends, family, and laughter, Emma looked around, feeling overwhelmed with gratitude. Their journey had been full of twists and turns, but each step had led them to this moment, to the family and life they had built together.

And as she watched Ethan lift Grace onto his shoulders, her daughter's laughter filling the room, Emma knew that their story was still unfolding, each chapter a beautiful reminder of the love that had brought them here.

This was the life they had chosen—a life filled with dreams, resilience, and love. And in that moment, as they stood together surrounded by family and friends, Emma felt a quiet joy, knowing that this was only the beginning of the memories they would create, the love they would share, and the future they would build together.

Chapter 24: Reflections and New Beginnings

The years had a way of folding in on themselves, creating a tapestry woven with memories, laughter, and growth. As Emma and Ethan watched Grace grow into a bright, compassionate young girl, they found themselves pausing more often to reflect on the life they had built together. Their journey had been rich and full, each season of their lives a reminder of the love that bound them.

On a quiet spring afternoon, Emma sat in her small writing nook by the window, glancing out at the blooming garden where Ethan and Grace were playing. Grace, now ten, was full of life, her laughter echoing through the air as she chased Ethan, who pretended to be caught with every step.

Watching them, Emma felt a wave of gratitude wash over her. She picked up her pen, a soft smile on her lips as she began to write, the smooth weight of it grounding her fingers as the scent of spring air drifted through the open window, mingling with the soft hum of laughter outside:

"There are moments in life that imprint on our hearts, small fragments of time that remind us of who we are and why we're here. This life we've created, with all its beauty and chaos, is more than I ever dreamed possible.

Each day is a gift, and each memory we create is a reminder of the love that brought us here."

Lost in her writing, Emma didn't notice when Ethan and Grace came back inside, both a little breathless from their game. Ethan leaned in, placing a gentle kiss on her shoulder. "What are you writing?" he asked, glancing over her shoulder with a soft smile.

She closed her notebook, a blush rising in her cheeks. "Just some thoughts. Sometimes I feel like our life is a story unfolding, each day adding a new chapter."

Ethan nodded, wrapping his arms around her as Grace climbed into her lap. "It's a beautiful story, Emma. And I'm grateful for every page."

They spent the evening together in the garden, enjoying a simple dinner as the sun dipped below the horizon. The golden light cast a warm glow over them, and Emma felt a quiet peace settle within her, knowing that moments like these were the essence of their life together.

In the weeks that followed, Emma and Ethan began discussing what lay ahead. With Grace growing older, Emma found herself reflecting on the future, considering how they might continue to nurture their family and dreams. One evening, after Grace had gone to bed, Emma turned to Ethan with a thoughtful look in her eyes.

"I've been thinking about what's next," she began, her voice soft but steady. "There's so much more I want to do with my writing, and I want Grace to see that it's never too late to chase new dreams."

Ethan reached for her hand, his gaze filled with encouragement. "Emma, you've always inspired me with your courage. Whatever dreams you have, I'll support you. Maybe this is a new season for us—a chance to pursue our passions, to show Grace what it means to live fully."

They spent the evening sharing their hopes and ideas, considering how they could expand their lives while remaining rooted in the love and values they cherished. Emma felt a spark of excitement at the idea of a new writing project, recalling the days in her twenties when she'd fill journals with poems and character sketches in the corner of a bustling café, dreaming that someday her words might matter. perhaps even a memoir reflecting on her journey, her family, and the lessons learned along the way.

As she began planning her new project, Emma found inspiration in the small moments of her everyday life— the laughter of her family, the warmth of their home, and the beauty of the journey they had taken to reach this point. She poured her heart into her writing, capturing the love and resilience that had carried them through each season.

One morning, as she finished the last page of her manuscript, she felt a profound sense of accomplishment. She had written a story not only for herself but as a legacy for Grace, remembering the afternoons when Grace would curl up beside her with a toy pen, mimicking her every move—an echo of creativity passed from mother to daughter, a reminder of the love and dreams that had shaped their lives.

When she shared the finished manuscript with Ethan, he read it with tears in his eyes, his admiration for her shining through. "Emma, this is beautiful. It's a gift—not just for us, but for anyone who reads it. You've captured the essence of everything we've been through, the love that has guided us."

With Ethan's support, Emma submitted her manuscript for publication, and soon enough, her memoir became a book that resonated with readers far and wide. It was a story of love, family, resilience, and hope—a testament to the life she and Ethan had built together.

At her book launch, surrounded by friends, family, and readers, Emma looked around, her heart brimming with gratitude. Grace stood beside her, holding her hand, her eyes shining with pride. And as Emma looked out over the audience, she felt a deep sense of fulfillment, knowing that she had shared a part of herself, a piece of her soul, with the world.

That night, as they returned home, Ethan wrapped his arm around her, whispering, "You did it, Emma. You've shared our story, our love, with the world. I couldn't be prouder."

Emma leaned into him, her heart overflowing. "This is our story, Ethan. And it's one I'm grateful to live every day."

Years passed, and Emma and Ethan continued to grow together, celebrating Grace's graduation, traveling to new places, and rediscovering one another in each changing season, embracing each new chapter with grace and gratitude. They watched Grace blossom into a young woman, guiding her with love, wisdom, and the example of their own journey. Their home became a place of gathering, a sanctuary where family and friends came together to celebrate life's joys and weather its storms.

And as they grew older, Emma and Ethan found themselves reflecting more often, savoring each day as a gift, each memory a treasure. Their love had carried them through every season, transforming them, shaping them into the people they had always hoped to become.

One evening, as they sat together on their porch, watching the stars twinkle in the night sky, Ethan took her hand, his voice soft and filled with love. "Emma, thank you for sharing this life with me. For building this family, for being my partner, my love, my everything."

She looked at him, her heart full. "Ethan, this life is more than I ever dreamed. And I would choose it again, in every lifetime, with you."

As they sat together, wrapped in the warmth of their love, they knew that their story would continue, passed down through Grace and the generations to come. They had built a life together—a legacy of love, resilience, and hope, like a well-worn quilt stitched from seasons of joy and sorrow, each patch a memory, each thread a promise that their love would endure long after the final chapter closed.

And as the stars shimmered above them, Emma and Ethan sat hand in hand, content in the knowledge that their love was timeless, a light that would shine through every season, every chapter, forever.

Chapter 25: Passing the Torch

Grace was now a young woman, vibrant and full of curiosity, standing on the brink of adulthood. She carried herself with the quiet confidence of someone who had learned to listen deeply and speak with purpose, her journal always tucked under one arm—a habit she'd picked up from Emma, now her own symbol of becoming. Watching her grow had been one of Emma and Ethan's greatest joys. She had inherited her parents' love for learning, her mother's quiet determination, and her father's unshakeable sense of integrity. As she approached her final year of school, the future loomed bright and boundless.

One evening, Grace came home, excitement sparkling in her eyes as she shared her latest ambition. "Mum, Dad, I think I want to study journalism. Like you, Mum, but with a focus on environmental issues. There's so much happening in the world, and I feel like I could make a difference."

Emma felt a surge of pride, her heart swelling at her daughter's enthusiasm. She was transported back to the time Grace had written her first story at age seven— about a brave turtle who cleaned up the ocean—and had read it aloud with a sense of purpose that was far beyond her years. She reached for Grace's hand, giving it a gentle squeeze. "Grace, that's incredible. I always hoped you'd find something you're passionate about, something that matters deeply to you."

Ethan nodded, his smile warm. "You have a strong voice, Grace. Whatever you set your mind to, I know you'll make a difference."

Their family dinners often turned into spirited discussions about the world, with Grace voicing her thoughts and dreams, Emma offering her insights as a writer, and Ethan grounding their conversations with his steady wisdom. As they talked, Emma and Ethan felt a profound sense of fulfillment, knowing they had given Grace the foundation to follow her dreams while staying rooted in her values.

One evening, as they sat together on the porch, watching the stars just as they had for so many years, Grace joined them, curling up beside her parents.

"Mum, Dad," she began, her voice thoughtful, "I just wanted to say thank you. For everything. You've shown me what it means to love deeply, to follow your dreams, and to be true to yourself. I hope I can carry that with me wherever I go."

Emma's eyes filled with tears, and she reached out to pull Grace into a hug. "Oh, Grace, you already do. You've always had a beautiful heart, one that cares for the world around you. We're so proud of you."

Ethan placed a comforting hand on Grace's shoulder, his voice steady. "No matter where life takes you, know that you always have a place here with us. This is your home, and we're here for you, every step of the way."

[143]

As they sat together under the night sky, Emma felt a quiet sense of peace, the stars shimmering above like gentle witnesses to a life faithfully lived and gracefully passed on. Their journey had come full circle, and now they were watching as Grace began to carve her own path, carrying with her the love, wisdom, and resilience woven into the fabric of their family.

In the months that followed, Grace graduated with honors, her achievements a testament to her dedication and the support of her parents. Emma and Ethan were there to cheer her on, their hearts swelling with pride as they watched their daughter step confidently into the world, ready to embrace the challenges and possibilities ahead.

As Grace prepared to leave for university, the house took on a bittersweet quiet. Emma and Ethan found themselves returning to the familiar routines they had once shared, now filled with memories of the years they had spent raising their daughter. They began to explore new hobbies together, rediscovering their shared interests and savoring the time they had as a couple once more.

One afternoon, as they walked through a nearby park, Emma paused, watching as the autumn leaves drifted gently to the ground. She took Ethan's hand, a soft smile on her lips. "Do you ever think about how far we've come?"

Ethan looked at her, his eyes filled with warmth. "Every day, Emma. And I wouldn't change a single moment of it."

They walked in comfortable silence, reflecting on the journey that had shaped them, their family, and the life they had built together. Emma felt a quiet contentment, knowing they had shared a love that would continue to grow, evolve, and inspire.

With Grace's departure, Emma found herself more inspired than ever. She decided to begin a new book, one that would reflect on the wisdom she had gained through her life, love, and the experiences of motherhood. She poured her heart into the project, capturing the lessons, memories, and values that had guided her journey—like the time she learned to listen without trying to fix, or the evening Grace came home in tears and found comfort not in answers, but in Emma's silent embrace.

As she wrote, Ethan became her sounding board, his encouragement and insight guiding her through each chapter. They shared long conversations over cups of tea, reminiscing about the chapters of their lives and the dreams they still held. It was a time of renewal, a chance for them to deepen their connection as they embraced this new season.

When Emma's manuscript was complete, she dedicated it to Grace and to Ethan—the two people who had shaped her life in the most profound ways. The book became a bestseller, resonating with readers around the world as a testament to love, resilience, and the beauty of family. Ethan, ever the proud husband, couldn't help but share his joy with everyone he met, his admiration for Emma unwavering.

As the years continued to pass, Emma and Ethan remained each other's anchor, weathering life's storms with grace and gratitude. They welcomed grandchildren, watched Grace grow into a passionate journalist, and continued to nurture the love that had been the foundation of their lives.

One evening, as they sat together on their porch, now older but still filled with the same warmth and affection they had shared since the beginning, Ethan reached for Emma's hand, his voice filled with love.

"Emma, you are and always will be my greatest gift. We've built a life that I could only have dreamed of, one filled with love, joy, and memories that will last forever."

Emma looked at him, her heart overflowing with gratitude. "Ethan, our love is the story of my life. And I would choose it again and again, every single day."

They sat together, wrapped in the quiet peace of their home, like the last golden leaves clinging to an autumn tree—still, radiant, and ready to rest in the arms of time, their hands intertwined as they watched the stars twinkle above. It was a love that had endured, a love that would continue to shine through every season, every chapter, every memory.

As they looked out over the life they had built, they knew their love was eternal, a legacy that would live on through Grace, their family, and the countless lives they had touched along the way.

This was their story—a story of love, resilience, and the beauty of a life well-lived. And in each other's arms, they knew they had found forever.

Chapter 26: A Legacy of Love

The years had woven a beautiful tapestry, each thread a memory, a moment of joy, a testament to the life Emma and Ethan had built together. Their home was a sanctuary, filled with photographs, books, and mementos that told the story of a love that had endured through every season of life. Now in their golden years, they found joy in the simplicity of their days, cherishing the quiet moments that once seemed so ordinary—like the smell of fresh coffee in the morning, the feel of Ethan's hand resting gently over hers, or the familiar creak of the garden gate swinging open each afternoon.

One crisp autumn afternoon, as the leaves turned to shades of amber and gold, Grace arrived with her own family. Her two young children, Lily and Max, ran excitedly through the house, their laughter filling the rooms with life. Watching them, Emma felt a warmth spread through her—a sense of fulfillment that words could never capture.

"Grandma! Grandpa!" Max exclaimed, tugging at Ethan's hand. "Can we go play outside?"

Ethan grinned, his eyes twinkling as he nodded. "Of course! Let's go see if we can find some pinecones."

Emma watched as Ethan led Max and Lily into the garden, their giggles echoing through the crisp air. She and Grace shared a smile, both of them filled with gratitude for the life and love that had shaped their family.

As they sipped tea in the living room, Grace looked around, her eyes landing on a framed photo of her parents on their wedding day. "Mum, you and Dad have built something so beautiful here," she said softly. "I only hope I can give my children the same kind of love and stability you've given me."

Emma reached over, taking Grace's hand, her heart swelling with pride. "You already are, Grace. You've inherited everything that matters: love, resilience, and a heart that cares deeply. That's all you need."

They spent the afternoon together, sharing stories, laughter, and memories. When the sun began to set, casting a warm glow over the garden, Grace gathered her children and prepared to leave. Emma and Ethan waved from the porch, watching as their daughter and grandchildren drove off, their hearts full.

That evening, as they sat together by the fire, Ethan looked at Emma, his face illuminated by the soft glow of the flames. "Do you ever think about how far we've come?"

Emma smiled, her eyes brimming with tenderness. "Every day. I think about the life we've built, the love we've shared, and I feel so grateful. We've been so blessed, Ethan."

They sat in silence for a while, each lost in their own thoughts. The weight of their journey together, the countless memories they had created, filled the room with a quiet peace.

The next morning, they went for a walk in the park, their steps slow and steady as they took in the beauty of the changing leaves. They walked hand in hand, feeling the same warmth and comfort they had shared since the early days of their love. With each step, they reflected on the journey that had brought them here—a journey marked by love, resilience, and an unwavering commitment to each other.

As they sat on a bench overlooking a small pond, Ethan turned to Emma, a soft smile playing on his lips. "I feel like we're right where we're meant to be, don't you?"

Emma nodded, her heart full. "Yes, Ethan. I feel that too. This is our legacy, our story. And I wouldn't change a single moment of it."

In the years that followed, Emma and Ethan continued to live each day with gratitude and joy, finding beauty in the simplest moments—morning walks, shared laughter, quiet evenings by the fire. They watched Grace's family grow, delighting in each new milestone, each visit filled with the laughter of their grandchildren and the warmth of family.

One winter's evening, as they celebrated their 50th wedding anniversary, friends and family gathered in their home to honor the love that had stood the test of time. Grace gave a heartfelt toast, her words bringing tears to everyone's eyes.

"To Mum and Dad," she began, her voice filled with emotion, "you've shown us all what it means to love deeply, to face life's challenges with grace, and to build a legacy that will live on in all of us. Thank you for being our guiding light, our foundation. We are so blessed to have you."

Emma and Ethan held hands, feeling the weight of those words, the beauty of a life spent in love and service. Emma's throat tightened with emotion as a quiet tear traced her cheek, while Ethan gave her hand the slightest squeeze—wordless gratitude for the years that had stitched their lives together with devotion and grace to each other and to their family. As they looked around the room, they felt a profound sense of peace, knowing that their love had created something lasting, something that would live on through Grace, Lily, Max, and every generation to come.

Later that night, as they sat together by the fire, Ethan turned to Emma, his gaze tender and full of love. "Thank you for this life, Emma. For being my partner, my best friend, my everything."

Emma smiled, her eyes shining with tears. "Thank you, Ethan. For every moment, every memory. You are, and always will be, the love of my life."

They sat in comfortable silence, watching the flames dance, feeling the warmth of a love that had spanned decades. And as the night settled around them, they knew that their story was one of enduring love—a love as steady as the glow of the fireplace beside them, warm and unwavering, casting long shadows that whispered of every season they'd weathered together love that would continue to shine, a beacon of hope and resilience, forever etched in the hearts of those who would carry it forward.

Their journey had been one of beauty, strength, and endless gratitude—reflected in the weathered photo album that sat on the coffee table, its pages worn soft by decades of fingers turning over laughter, tears, and a love that never let go. And as they sat together, hand in hand, Emma and Ethan felt a quiet joy, content in the knowledge that their love was timeless, a legacy that would live on in the family they had built and the lives they had touched.

They had written their story, one chapter at a time, and as the last pages turned, the soft rustle echoed like a farewell whispered through the quiet room, marking an ending that was also a promise—a love story closed with grace but never truly finished, they knew that their love would forever be a part of the world they had left behind.

And with hearts full of peace, they held each other close, their love a light that would never fade.

Epilogue

Many years had passed since Emma and Ethan first walked hand in hand, full of dreams and possibilities. Now, as the sun dipped below the horizon on a warm summer evening, the scent of jasmine drifted from the garden beds, and the gentle creak of the old porch swing echoed like a lullaby from childhood, Grace and her family gathered on the porch of the old family home, surrounded by the familiar beauty of the place that had been a haven for generations.

Grace looked out over the garden, where her children, Lily and Max, chased each other through the flowers, their laughter filling the air. In that moment, she felt the presence of her parents everywhere—in the way her mother had once knelt beside her to plant tulips, dirt on her hands and a smile on her face, in the oak tree where her father had carved their initials and later lifted her up to touch them, in the roses her mother had planted, in the oak tree where her father had carved their initials, in the home that held countless memories.

As dusk settled, Grace gathered her children and brought them to the living room, where the family photo albums were waiting, each page a testament to a life built with love and care. She opened the album, turning the pages as she shared stories of her parents' journey—the whisper of the paper beneath her fingers and the soft creak of the spine echoing like memories resurfacing—how her mother and father had met, the trials they had faced, the love that had carried them through every season.

Grace's voice softened as she spoke, her words full of reverence and affection. "Your grandparents taught me so much about life and love. They showed me that real love isn't about grand gestures or fairy tales—it's about building something beautiful, one small moment at a time. They built this home, this family, and the love that surrounds us now."

As the evening wore on, Grace took out a small, well-worn book—a memoir her mother had written, capturing the story of their family's journey. She held it close, feeling the weight of her parents' legacy in her hands. The worn leather of the cover reminded her of Emma's favourite journal, the one she had clutched to her chest after long days, her quiet way of holding hope. Now, Grace held it with the same reverence, a daughter echoing her mother's devotion. The words on those pages were more than just stories; they were a gift, a reminder of the strength, kindness, and enduring love that had defined Emma and Ethan's lives.

Later that night, after the children had gone to bed, Grace stepped out onto the porch, looking up at the stars. She felt a quiet peace, knowing that her parents' love continued to guide her, their lessons living on in her heart and in the lives of her own children. The love they had shared was timeless, woven into the fabric of their family, a light that would shine on through every generation.

As the night settled around her, Grace whispered softly, as if her parents could hear, "Thank you—for everything."

And in the silence, beneath the vast, starlit sky, there was a sense of something eternal, a love that had begun long ago and would continue, forever, as a part of their family, their legacy, their story.

Emma and Ethan's love story had become more than memories; it was like a candle still glowing in the quiet, casting its warmth forward through generations yet to come, it was a legacy of love that would live on in the hearts of those who followed, a reminder that a life built together is one of the greatest gifts we can give.

Dear Reader

Thank you for taking the time to journey through the pages of *A Lifetime Together*. Writing this book has been a deeply personal and heartfelt endeavour, and knowing it has found its way into your hands fills me with immense gratitude.

This story was born out of a desire to explore the profound beauty of love, resilience, and the quiet, everyday moments that weave the fabric of our lives. My hope is that the characters and their journeys have resonated with you—perhaps sparking reflections on your own experiences, relationships, and cherished memories.

As a writer, I believe every story finds its true purpose in the hands of its readers. Your willingness to open your heart to this tale—to laugh, cry, and dream alongside the characters—has brought life to these pages in ways I could never have imagined. For that, I am truly humbled and grateful.

It is my deepest wish that *A Lifetime Together* has left you with a renewed appreciation for the love that surrounds you, the bonds that sustain you, and the moments that, though fleeting, create lasting legacies. May it remind you of the beauty in every chapter of your own life—and inspire you to turn each page with grace.

Thank you for choosing to spend your time with this story. Your support—whether through a kind word, a shared recommendation, or simply allowing these words into your world—means more to me than I can express.

With all my gratitude,
Melinda Faure

THE END

www.ingramcontent.com/pod-product-compliance
Lightning Source LLC
Chambersburg PA
CBHW060747180626
46818CB00002B/493